BEARMOUTH

Norton Young Readers

An Imprint of W. W. Norton & Company
Independent Publishers Since 1923

BEARMOUTH

LIZ HYDER

For information about permission to reproduce selections from this book,
write to Permissions, W. W. Norton & Company, Inc.,
500 Fifth Avenue, New York, NY 10110

For information about special discounts for bulk purchases, please contact
W. W. Norton Special Sales at specialsales@wwnorton.com or 800-233-4830

Manufacturing by Lake Book Manufacturing
Book design by Beth Steidle
Production manager: Beth Steidle

Library of Congress Cataloging-in-Publication Data

Names: Hyder, Liz, author.
Title: Bearmouth / Liz Hyder.
Description: First American edition. | New York : Norton Young Readers,
2020. | Originally published: London : Pushkin Children's Books, 2019. |
Audience: Ages 13–18. | Summary: Having lived and worked in Bearmouth
mine since age four, Newt accepts everything about the brutal life until
mysterious Devlin arrives and dares to ask why, leading Newt and other
miners to challenge the system.
Identifiers: LCCN 2020018577 | ISBN 9781324015864 (hardcover) |
ISBN 9781324015871 (epub)
Subjects: CYAC: Coal mines and mining—Fiction. | Child labor—Fiction. |
Revolutions—Fiction.
Classification: LCC PZ7.1.H9175 Be 2020 | DDC [Fic]—dc23
LC record available at https://lccn.loc.gov/2020018577

W. W. Norton & Company, Inc., 500 Fifth Avenue, New York, N.Y. 10110
www.wwnorton.com

W. W. Norton & Company Ltd., 15 Carlisle Street, London W1D 3BS

1 2 3 4 5 6 7 8 9 0

BEARMOUTH

In the beginnin there was the Mayker

An he mayde all around us

He mayde all the men an all the wimmin

He mayde all the creetures on this, his Earf

The Mayker loved each and evryone o us

But then all us men an wimmin betrayd him

They took his Trust an spatt on it

An the Mayker was angry

He sent us down into the dark Earf

To atone for the sins o our forefarvers an muvvers

An one day, tis sed, the Mayker will give us a sine

We will all be foregivven

An we will rise up to the land

An the lyte that the Mayker holds there in his parm

Will be givern to all o us

An all shall prosper in this life an the next

Amen.

I AM LERNIN MY LETTUZ

I am lernin mi letterz
I am lerrnin my lettiss

I am lernin my letterz.
I am learnin my letters.

Better, says Thomas as he blows out the lyte.

TIS HARD WORK USIN MY BRAYNE.

Thomas teeches me at lunch when the uvvers are at caban an sometimes on Maykers Day I have lessuns arfter prayers.

In the week, the men sit an diskuss things for grown ups at caban an us youngs arnt alloud in. Menstalk they say. Not for youngs.

So I sits out here wi Thomas an he teeches me my letters. They are hard. Only me an Tobe are learnin letters. The rest are too old. Tobe is more young than me but he learns fast an all.

Thomas is my best frend tho hes twyce my ayge an more. He looks arfter me, keeps an eye out. I am diffrent see. I am not one thing or the uvver. They call me YouNuck for I am not a boy nor yet a wimmin an they hold no truck for gels down here so I must by all akkounts be a YouNuck. Not one thing or the uvver. Thomas dunt lyke them calling me that tho so he calls me Newt.

En ee double yoo tee. Newt.

I lyke that.

Thomas says its an undergrawnd creeture, small an nimball. Lyke me.

Learnin letters is hard. My eyes strayne at the end o lessun wi the bryteness o the candul lyte. Then tis back to work for all three o us.

10

BEARMOUTH IS MY HOME SEE. Tis calld Bearmouth cos it was near the surfiss wi its wyde open maw so us could walk strayte into the mine but then they dug down, deeper an deeper, myles an myles down, so we are toastee warm at work. So tis the wrong nayme now. Bearmouths are for shallow mines an we ent that. It should be calld Black Pit. Or center o the earf.

When I first cayme, I was a trapper see. Baysic rayte o not very much coinage but an important job shore. Lettin the air in an out, openin doors for ponys an the rest.

Now I am a trayler workin to my hagger. We are a team me an Jack. He shouts at me when I am not fast enuff. He cuts wi his mandril an I packs an moves it.

A trayler has a hole nuvver langwidge you must learn fast. When I startd, I knew nun o it but Jack teeched me. He says Im smart. He dunt kno his letters at all. But he can count. An he works fast. Very fast. Sometimes tis hard to keep up wi him. But the more we cuts, the more we earns.

I earn more being a trayler. One day Ill be a hagger too, lyke Jack.

I gets fiffteen at the moment. Haggers gets more lyke sixtee wuld you believe.

I can do my job blindfold pretty much.

Which is a good thin cos it sayves on canduls.

Canduls are spensive.

I spends fyve on canduls evry week. Fyve on food an

matchiss, two on hot water an the rest. Which leeves three wot I sends to Ma.

I ent seen Ma an the rest since I cayme here. Maykers Day ent long enuff to get there an back arfter prayers an the lyke. An I only has that one day a week.

It taykes most harf a day to get back up there, to the surfiss. An it costs. Thirtee each way cos o the lift sharft. So I stays here. Tis cheeper in the dark. I ent seen daylyte since I was fore. Not shore how long ago that were in all trooth but it feels a long time since.

Bein a trayler is tuff but it helps me learn my letters. See, when I pushs the basket to an fro from tram to main road, up the inklyne, in the heat an the dust an dark, I goes over the letters in my head.

WHEN WE FINISHES TODAY, THERE IS A NEW BOY IN GAMBLES BUNK. He lays there all day an cry cryes in the corner til Jack slaps him an tells him to shuddup an keep choired so we could get some sleep.

Gamble died last week. Blown up silly bugger an then Harrison got it an all from the vapours tryin to rescue him. Arfterdamp can kill they say. An it did for Harrison.

Two emptee beds.

Now just one.

The new boy looks so spinky clene see. Lyke a newborn foal.

His eyes are massiv. He looks frytend too. Petryfyed.

He ent sed a word.

ON FIRST SHIFT, THE NEW LAD SHIVERS BY THE DOORS FROM TRAM TO MAIN ROAD. Trappin. Nicholson is teechin him wot to do but hes twyce the ryte ayge an more, an he ent goin to be sayvin much coinage if hes usin up canduls at a rayte o nots.

Neether the new lad nor Nicholson are in the mood for talkin. Tis black as nyte but I can hear the new lad holdin his tears in.

When I sees him layter, at end time arfter shifts, they hav slit his nose. The ryte nostril. Lyke they always do. See if yore man enuff to work. A sharp peece o stone see, zip, strayte up. If you cryes, they beats you.

We all got the scar. Tis how you kno yore a Bearmouth boy.

Hes one o us now. Whevver he wants it or not.

THOMAS SAYS THE NEW BOY IS CALLD DEVLIN.

I ent herd him talk as yet but Thomas is good at gettin
stuff out o folk. He listerns. Waytes til folk have summat
to say an then listerns to them. He says he could o bin a
learned man an I believe him. Hes the most learned man
I ever met.

Devlin.

Devil In.

We ent bin spectin anyone new down here speshully not
a young lad. I ent shore about him. We should be cayreful.
Maybe his nayme is a warnin. He is handsum enuff. Devil in
disguys. He myte lead us to temptayshun. I pray xtra hard to
the Mayker to sayve us.

To keep vigil over us.

An to keep speshul watch on Devlin. Mayker protekt me.

He dunt cry no more tho Devlin. Not now. Hes bin here
most o a week an he dos have a steely look now. Eyes as black
as the coal we digs out. Hard an tuff lyke Jack says you got
to be.

I think o wot he says to me earlier. Devlin. Whisperin,
lyke a spyder tippy toein along a wall.

It only taykes one person to start it, he says, voyce ticklin
my ears. Just one.

Wot? Start wot? I whispers back as I pushs my load past
the trap hes holdin open for me.

A revolushun, he says. Just one, he says. Think on that.

I hear his smyle in the darkness. I feels him shut the

door behind me an the breeze blows ryte down my neck an maykes me shudder.

I asks Thomas at letters what (double yoo haytch ay tee, he says) revolushun meens, he tells me ryte off to keep my voyce down. He says I durnt say such things out loud. Not even think em. Not even whisper.

Layters he says to me what it ment. Rebellion. Disobeyin. I think about the Mayker. He sees evrythin. He knos evrythin. If the Mayker sees rebellion, he will skwash it lyke an ant. Lyke Jack did that baby mouse in my bed that time. Skwish skwash flat. Tis the Maykers will. Tis always the Maykers will. I prays xtra hard to be sayved.

Mayker protekt me. Mayker protekt us all. Amen.

TODAY IS MAYKERS DAY. Tis the first Sunday we has had Devlin here. I ent talked to him since before. I dunt want my ears poysoned wi talk o revolushun an the lyke. Speshully not on Maykers Day.

Sundays are speshul.

We gets up layters an has brekfast in the mess wi sum o those from the uvver parts o Bearmouth that we dunt normally see cos they is on diffrent shifts. But here we are. Crammd in together on long benches in the whitewashd hall. Most days we have gruel wi salt but on Maykers Day we hav shuggar. It taystes so diffrent, so sweete an lovelee that I holds my bowl up an drinks it down in one go. Then I licks my finger an wypes the bowl spinky clene.

Thomas larfs at me for being so greedee an Jack tells me off for havin no manners. Devlin watches. Choiredly. Waytes for evryone else to finish fore he eats his, slowlee, wi a spoon. He taykes so long that Jack nicks his bowl fore hes harfway throo.

Here YouNuck, he says, finish this lads off will ya. Hes taykin so long I fear he dunt lyke the tayste!

All the men larf too. But Devlin ent larfin. Hes sat there, starin at me. I could eat anuvver fyve bowls o the stuff, trooth be told, but this is anuvver lads bowl. That goes gainst evrythin.

I dunt say nuffink, but I shaykes my head.

Thomas spekes for me. Ent calld YouNuck, nayme o Newt, he says firm lyke.

Jack ignores him. He narrows his eyes at me an downs the bowl hisself, slappin it down on the tayble arfter, when hes empteed it.

Devlin just sits there, watchin me. Watchin Jack. I feel unsettld, funny in my belly. I dunt meet Devlins eye til just fore the canduls are blown out an Im shore I see his lips curl, almost lyke a smyle. The Devils smyle.

Mayker sayve an protekt me.

We walks up the portways to the levels above, one, two, I counts em on my fingers lyke Thomas tort me. As we goes higher up, the air becomes more chill. Three, fore. I dunt lykes it up here. The winds an the breeze, lyke ghosts ticklin. But we has to come up. Tis where we thank the Mayker. For our lives, for our daylee bred, for evrythin.

Fyve. Past the guards standin watch.

Six.

It taykes ayges. As it always dos. Uphill in the dark, just followin the sounds in front o you. The tracks are larger up here, taller an wyder an you dunt have to stoop to mind yore head so often.

Severn, ayte.

Finally, nyne an then ten. The Maykers here. All over this level. Evrywhere. You feels him all round you in the air, in the lyte. Canduls flicker an burn wherere you look. Tis bryte. So bryte. Hurts my eyes. I blinks an blinks an tears come into my eyes. Tis the sayme evry Sunday. The bryteness o the Mayker. Showin us the way. Guidin us wi his lytes so bryte it will blind if you looks at em for too long.

We walks up a short flyte o stairs, carved out o the rock an whitewashd to reflekt the lytes o the canduls an then turn ryte throo the wyde doorway an into the grayte Hall where the Mayker is. The canduls flicker as we walks into his Hall an joins all the uvver hundreds o men an lads from the uvver parts o Bearmouth.

The Maykers Hall dos fayre tayke my breath away. Evry Maykers Day tis the sayme but I feels my heart beats faster an a lyteness o body when I comes in here. Tis solid rock is the Hall an the biggest room I ever did see. On one side, opposit where we enters an leeves see, theres ruff stone in the shaype o a giant, a god to oversee us. The Mayker hisself. Some say tis always bin there, uvvers say it was carvd but theres a fayce in it. Ryte high at the top, a fayce looking down at you. If you skwints, you sees it better.

I tryes not to look at it anymore. It frytens me. That hes here. The Mayker. That hes here mongst us. Mayker sayve us.

Afore we sings, we says the prayer. We says it evryday when we gets up. But here tis led by Missta Sharp. Hes the overseer on akkount o him overseein things, our work, our wellfayre, the hole workins o the mine. He ent in charge tho, he dunt own the mine, thats the Master, Missta Johnson that is. I ent ever seen him but I hears once that he is tall an thin an wears funny clothes wi a tall hat on his head. All shiny blue an spinky clene lyke the sky mayde solid.

But I am distrakted. Thomas says I am eesily distrakted. Devlin stands next to me, I feels him there, even wi out lookin. The heat comes off him lyke a cloud. The darkness teeches you that. How to read someone wi out seein em.

I joins in the prayer. Chantin, chantin.

In the beginnin there was the Mayker
An he mayde all around us
He mayde ull the men an all the wimmin

He mayde all the creetures on this, his Earf
The Mayker loved each an evryone o us
But then all us men an wimmin betrayd him
They took his Trust an spatt on it
An the Mayker was angry
He sent us down into the dark Earf
To atone for the sins o our forefarvers an muvvers
An one day, tis sed, the Mayker will give us a sine
We will all be foregivven
An we will rise up to the land
An the lyte that the Mayker holds there in his parm
Will be givern to all o us
An all shall prosper in this life an the next

Amen.

Devlin is silent. He dunt join in. Dunt even mouthe the words silently lyke I used to fore I learnt em all.

Hes got a faraway look on his fayce. Lyke hes somewhere else entirelee. Maybe he too is eesily distrakted.

When we starts to sing, I feels him lookin at me. It taykes all my willpower not to look back but insted I turns to look up at the Mayker, I looks up at his rock fayce an sings an sings to him an I dunt dare look away til my neck aykes an tis time to go.

20

ON MAYKERS DAY WE ARE ALLOUD A SPESHUL TREAT. We are
alloud to swim in the layke for harf a coin. We wash there,
arfter work, both body an clothes by the pumps that pump
the water up up an over us an back down to the layke. But
we ent alloud to swim in it not lest we fall in by axident.
But Maykers Day tis a speshul day. Still, we has to paye for
it lykes we have to paye for most things. Boots, canduls,
clothes an the lyke.

Not evryone lykes swimmin. Jack dunt lyke it, says tis
unnatchural, but Thomas an I do an Tobe too. We dunt do
it evry Maykers Day cos o the cost but when we can, we do.
Xtra speshul. Spinky clene.

When we was really little, smaller than we are now, me
an Tobe used to swim round the hole edge o the layke, in
the dark, tryin to find cayves an tunnels. But we stoppd
when Jack told us about the day that two men drownd when
they was xplorin. They disappeerd for three days an then
their bloatd bodies was found, float floatin on the layke.
Jack reckons they found a tunnel an tryd to swim throo but
got stuck.

Thomas dunt agree tho. He says to me there was marks
round the mens necks. Lyke someone had dun em in. He
says they was trubble an someone did for em. He never
mentshund it again tho so part o me thinks I did magine it.

Tomorro is payday an most folk have run clene out o
munny. But Thomas an Tobe an me, we keep our harf coin
sayved up when we cun for a Maykers Day swim. Tis our

treet. We spend most all arfternoon there arfter prayers.
Thomas maykes me an Tobe go over an over our letters too.
Spellin things out loud, hearin our voyces echo around
the cavern. Tis odd hearin ourselves lyke that. Our voyces,
disembodeed, call callin back at us.

I knos it lyke the backs o my hand now. The layke. Lyke
my floor in the mine, my level. I can walks it backwuds
blindfold an Id still kno it. Funny spreshun, the back o
yore hand. Oft I carnt see me hands in front o me when Im
workin lest I lyte a candul an I tryes an sayves em for when
I need em most. The blackness is all around, hole.

I carnt believe my eyes nor ears when Devlin comes in.
I hears him fore I sees him. Shufflin, uncertin, maykin a
grayte load o noyse wi a lit candul in his hand an all. Wastin
a lyte. Im alreddy in deep in the water by this poynte. Just
my head bobbin above. The rest o me free. Floatin. I can
feel the white fish nibble my tose. Thomas says they be
blind, the fish, but I lykes the feel o em ticklin me. Tis all
spoyled tho wi the Devil here. Tis our treet, tis for us not
for him. Devil In.

Whats he doin here? I says sharp. He dunt even get payd
til tomorro for his first week.

Choired, little one, says Thomas. Beehave yoreself.
Is this how you welcome our new frend? I lent him the
munny, says Thomas an I pulls a fayce at him. Waystin harf a
coin on a lad you dunt even kno. Spoylin our layke day.

I dives under the water, cool an calmin, to soothe my
angry hot fayce. As I comes back up, I hears Thomas talkin
in a low voyce to him.

Hotheaded, he says, but the most loyal frend you could
have. Smart too.

Hes talkin bout me.

Then Thomass voyce drops too low for ears an they talks more. I swims closer, choired as one o the fish, but he braykes off.

Thomas sits on the rocks, nayked as a seal bar his unders, skin rich an smooth an burnishd brown as Devlins candul flickers by him, burnin down. Devlin slowly taykes his clothes off too. First, his shirt, grey wi dust an then his boots an socks. Nayked to the waist. I stares at him. Hes beautiful, all muscle an lyte. But there are bruses too, big grey streeks lyke the coal seams we search for. Carnt be from this week when he was just trappin, sat openin an shuttin the door for air flo. From what then? He sees me watchin an turns his back, fayce flaymin wi embarassment. I shrugs to myself. What dos it matter? The Mayker mayde us all in his image. Tis his will.

As he turns his back on me, I sees more. Scars still healin, grayte scarlet lynes o weals scored down his back. Lyke that time Tobe was whipped for disobeedients an I had to wash his back evry day for a hole week fore it stopped bleedin.

Devlin pulls his trowsers down then his unders an there he is, back to me, buttocks smooth an creamee an as nayked as the day he come into the world an nayked as the day he will be returnd to the Mayker.

I find myself blush—Mayker forgive me—as he turns around to fayce me an I ducks my head in the water, but not fore I glimpses him. White an dry an coal dark eyes. His skin glows in the candul lyte. Trooth be told tis the most handsum thing I ever did clap my eyes on. I blush at the sinfull thawt—an on Maykers Day too.

I dives deep deep down until my cheeks feel less hot. An then hes beside me. In the water, splish splash sploshin. Not

elegant an choired. Not lyke a seal or a fish. Lyke a grayte
lumpen dog causin waves an froth.

This feels so good, he says out loud. This feels so good!
He gives a yelp as he dives down, feet in the air, an I almost
smyles but insted I remoov myself from temptayshun an
clambers out onto the rock. I sits next to Thomas an wrings
myself out, drip drip onto my nees. I pulls my soppin wet
unders up an all. Most o the men dunt wear unders harf
the time but Thomas told me an Tobe we should always
wear some even when we washes under the pumps or goes
swimmin see. Thomas dos the sayme an I kno some think its
odd but tis how it is.

What was you talkin about? I says.

Thomas just looks at me, eyes harf closed, a sleepy smyle
on his fayce.

Nothin, he says.

But I kno that ent troo.

Hes dayngeruss, I whisper to Thomas. Dayngeruss.

Thomas sits immobile. Opens one eye an looks at me.

People are only as dayngeruss as you give em leeve to be,
little one. An Thomas shuts his eye again.

Sometimes I think Thomas can see into my sole, lyke
the Mayker hisself. Cross, I move further away to dry off
before I pull my clothes back on again. They feel scratchy
an wrong. I stomps all the way back to my bunk an sulks for
what feels lyke the rest o the day.

TOBES BIN KEEPIN SEEKRETS. I kno this cos I found him out see. Hes bin actin straynge in dorm a few nytes fore lytes out, lyke he dos have flees or summat. Wriggall wriggall. But it ent flees I kno now.

Turns out soppy bugger bin feedin an befrendin a mouse o all things. I ent shore tis a mouse as seems awfull big for one. Tis a rat I swears by it but it dos seem tayme enuff an Tobe is awfull fond o it. He calls it Mouse an I am sworn to silence on it as Tobe mayde me do so. We ent alloud pets in Bearmouth see. An mice ent xactly the cleenest o creetures.

Mouse wud be for the chop if any uvvers found out about it so I crosses my parm an promisses I ent tellin but I dos tell Tobe that he needs must be cayreful o keepin Mouse hidden aways. He dos nod an agree but he ent cayreful enuff. An so Mouse dos lead us both into trubble.

Tis payday today see an tis always kayoss. We gets payd once a month on a Munday. The men are alloud beer fore they gets their wayges, drinkin their earnins away fore coinage even hits their pockit. In the mess, beer is brawt down in grayte barrels, hevvier than the basket I pushs up the rails evry day. Rolly rolly in they come, grayte big barrels longer than me. Taps are pushd onto em an the beer poors out lyke grayte streams o piss. Not cheep neether. A man could drink a weeks coinage an more on Beer Munday.

Jacks bin ill wi it once or twyce. Once he was so ill that

I had to cut an haul, he sed he wuld pay me for it twyce over but he never. Used to clip me round the ear if I wunt fast enuff, a proper cuff, but he ent dun that since so I spose I did earn somethin from it.

Theres power in the air on payday. You feels it cracklin, whisslin down the sharfts an tunnels. Tis dayngeruss, lyke one spark could lyte up the hole mine. Us youngs steer cleer o the men when they come back layte. A long time ago, when I was proper little, Harrison come back drunk an tryes to climb into bed wi me. I dunt really remember it but I remember Thomas give him a black eye for it. I dint mind too much when Harrison snuffd it too. I never lyked him overly. Still I wunt wish arfterdamp vapours on none, not even worst enemees. Suffokaytin in the dark cos o poyson gases. Tis the worst way to go.

Payday maykes me nervuss see. All that power cracklin around Bearmouth. An today me an Tobe seen summat that I am shore as shore can be that we wunt sposed to an now we both needs must keep annuver seekret.

Arfter letters, me an Tobe is headin back to work an Mouse wriggalls out o Tobes pockit.

Let him go, I says holdin Tobe back as Mouse skurrys off but he twists free o me an goes arfter. I carnt affords to be layte back to shift else Jack will lose his temper but I follows arfter Tobe anyways, mutterin stewpid Mouse to myself.

I follows Tobes candul flick flickrin round corners an downhill past the barrear that we ent sposed to go past cos it dos denote a part we ent alloud in no more. Dead passidges they calls it when all has bin rippd from its core an there ent no more black gold for the taykin. Two more corners round an I sees him stoopd in a corner an scoopin up that blastd Mouse.

Hurry up, I hisses but I hears someone comin so I runs over an blows out his lyte.

If we are cawt here there be trubble, tis out o bowndes. I holds Tobe close to me in the dark, feelin his heart beat beatin.

Shh, I whispers. I feels him nod, claspin Mouse tyte to his chest.

A lyte flick flickers further down the dead passidge. Ent no uvver sposed to be down here see. I hears voyces now too.

Shh, I says to Tobe an I holds my finger to his lips.

I creeps forwud tip toein down the passidge towards the voyces wi my arms out feelin my way in the dark. Who else myte be down here? I is thinkin. Tobe reetches for my hand an we both edges forwud towards the lyte.

We shud go back, says Tobe whisperin.

Wayte, I says. Shh.

I creeps forwud til I can just about see round the corner. I inches an peeks out behind the support post clutchin it wi my hand, nayles diggin into the musty wood. I peeks down the narrow passidge an there is a man on his nees, candul lyte flickrin on him. I sees his fayce cos he is lookin up lyke but I dunt kno him. He ent famileear to me.

I straynes to hear what he says but tis cleer he is upset, harf sobbin, his fayce is all batterd.

Please, he says. Please.

Anuvver man what I carnt see hits him hard about the fayce. Theres a shadow o a third man in the candul lyte.

It ent what you think, says the man on his nees. Blood dos run from his nose. Tis just talk is all. I ent dun nuffink wrong.

He gets hit again for that. Whakk round his hed.
I winces at the sound o it.

Cayreless talk, says the man in the shadows. Rylin the uvvers. Gettin em workd up. We carnt have that now can we Rickerbee? Carnt have awkwud men here. Gatherin is forebidden outside o mess an dorms, ent we told you that afore?

There wunt be no trubble no more, says the man they calls Rickerbee, snifflin lyke.

No, says the shadow man. No there wunt. No groups, no gatherin, no talk, no disobeedients. Mayke him learn his lessun, he says to the man doin all the hittin an he goes in again on him.

Rickerbee cryes out but there ent none to hear him, sayve me an Tobe.

Banish me, he says tween blows. Banish me as an awkwud man.

Oh yule be banishd alryte, says the voyce in the shadows. Theres time enuff for that yet. Carry on, he says to the fella as the fists rain down on Rickerbee.

Mayker sayve us. Tis lyke they meen to batter him to his last breath an there ent nothin I can do. We carnt keep watchin tho—this ent for youngs. My foot slips an kicks a rock, echoin as it rolleys down the passidge. I holds my breath.

Hello, says the voyce from the shadows. Anyone there?

Me an Tobe we skuttles out o there faster than a hayre, runnin past the barrear an back into Bearmouth proper. I pulls Tobe behind me, heart in mouth, draggin him fayre back to our dorm, taykin evry twist an turn I can. When Im shore we ent followd, we stops, pantin an out o breath.

We carnt say nuffink about this, I says to Tobe in a low voyce. We ent seen or herd nuffink.

He nods.

I meens it, I says. We got to get back to work sharpish
lyke an we ent never talkin bout it again. Got it?

He nods.

If Mouse runs off again, you lets him. Got that too?

He nods, eyes wyde.

I pats his head fore he goes. Got to keep an eye on Tobe
see. Got to keep an eye out for the youngest.

I catch my breath fore I heads back down to Jack.
Rules is rules. Things is how they is. Dunt step out o lyne.
Keep yore head down. Work hard an yule get yore reward.
I repeets em to myself as I gets back to work an Jack kicks me
in the shins for bein layte.

Mayker protekt me, I works so hard the rest o the day
that tis lyke I fayre dreamd that man Rickerbee. I durnt dare
think o it so I puts it to the back o my mind. There ent no
Rickerbee, I says over an over. There ent no shadow man.
But there is. I kno there is. I seen em both.

I prays xtra hard to the Mayker to sayve us all.

ARFTER WORK ON PAYDAY, THE MEN WASHS AN GETS TO MESS FAST AS THEY CAN. Sometimes tis the fastest you see em. All dashin an jolly an hungree for the taste o beer. Nicholson, Skillen an Jack is larfin an slappin each uvver on the back as they dryes off arfter wash, fired up by thawt o beer. Will an Joe are mewt as they always is but there eyes are fayre lit up. When we washes by the layke, I keeps my eyes out for Rickerbee by the pumps but I kno he ent workin in this part o the mine as I ent never clappd eyes on him afore today. Still I looks tho. Just in cayse.

Thomas dos not partayke o the drinkin an us youngs arnt alloud anyways. I dunt lykes the smell o it neether. Maykes me feel kweasee. Devlin must be nearly old enuff to go but he stays wi Thomas an us. Sted o drinkin beer, we sit in caban insted where the men sits an eats their lunch. Tis lyke a shack in the rocks where a dozen men or so can rests a while but us youngs ent normally alloud in. Caban has benches see, nycer than mess taybles. Tis snug in there too, warm in the belly o the mine. I sees Tobe clasp Mouse tyte to him in his pockit so not even Thomas knos hes there.

Payday tis the only time we is alloud in caban, when no folk knos an none can see us. Thomas tells us storyes an sometimes we maykes one up together, the three o us, magicks it up out o thin air. Tales o draguns an witches an cooldrons an potent brews lyke the beer they drinks above our heads two levels up.

Today is diffrent tho cos <u>he</u> is here. I wish Devlin wuld go away, leeve us alone. I wish he ent never come here. Thomas is my frend, myne an Tobes, an I dunt want to shayre him. The three o us are tyte see, tyter than a not on a string. An since <u>he</u> arrived, I feels things unravellin slowly slowly lyke a bootlayce comin all undun. I think o what me an Tobe saw earlier, the man in the shadows, an I shudders.

I dunt want to mayke up a story when Devlins here. What if he larfs at Tobe? What if he is meen to us, bout our storyes? Maybe he thinks there babeeish. I sit there wi arms crossed an eyes narrowd, silent.

Letters an storyes are important, Thomas says. So as you can read an ryte an share yore views an ideas an thawts.

Why ent you in caban normally? Devlin asks Thomas an we all go choired for a bit.

Thomas lykes to shayre his learnedness, I says firm lyke. Thass all. Which is harf the trooth at leest. Thomas is diffrent too see. He says to me once that he had to fyte his way out o trubble a few times when he first cayme. Speke wi his fists on akkount o the fact men looked at him diffrent cos o his darker skin. We ent never spoke about it since. I ent talkin bout it to Devlin thass for shore. Thomas says nothin for a bit, deep in thawt, an then he starts tellin a story, lyke he dos. Once upon a time they always starts. An then a story lyke the Maykers Prayer but longer an, Mayker forgive me, better an all.

Todays is about three children wi our naymes—Tobe, Newt an Devlin. Three children lost in a forest, deep in the deep dark woods wi branches twistin an twirlin above em. In the distance, a gingerbred house, mayde o sweete things, lykes o which I can barely magine. Shuggar twisted into canes lyke a walkin stik an a thing calld choclit, dark brown sweetniss that dos melt in the mouth. I licks my lips an my mouth waters at the thawt o it. I wypes it wi the end o my sleeve.

A witch lives in the sweete house, says Thomas, but she pretends to be a nyce lady an tells the three children to come in. A bite to eat an a rest, she says but then she locks em up, keys an chains, for her own supper.

She plans to eat em? says Tobe eyes wyde wi horror.

Devlin smirks at this poynte an I want so hard to wype it from his fayce I almost bursts but Thomas, he carnt abyde violence these days so I sayves my temper an shoves it back into a small angry ball deep down inside.

Corse the story ends up as Thomass storyes always do wi a happy endin. The three o us kills the witch, throws her onto the fire an woosh she disappeers in smoke up the chimnee, burns to little smitty bits o soot an we lives happly ever arfter in her house.

I carnt see me an Devlin livin happly ever arfter even wi Tobe there to keep the peace but I keeps my trap shut an stay silent.

Why dyou mayke up these storyes? says Devlin. Why dyou mayke em up? Theyre fayree tales for ones smaller than these.

Thomas turns to him, thawtful lyke. It passes the time, he says. Tis tales o dreams an hopes. What is man if he cannot dream? If he cannot use his maginayshun to brayke free o a fysical cayge? What is man if he cannot hope?

Devlin looks down, lyke hes ashaymd. Thomas has wyse words that he pores out, sometimes I dunt understand em all but I lykes listernin to the words flow from him lyke the small waterfall at the back o the layke.

Too soon our time in caban is over an we traypse back to dorm where the beerfilld men snore an snort lyke wild pigs.

32

Nothin waykes em when theyre lyke this. Thomas says theyve drunk their earnins away, tomorros piss.

I lies in bed tryin not to think about Devlin. One, two, three, fore beds down. I wishes him away, eyes tytely shut.

I thinks o the shadow man too, who he is an where he is now.

Tis alryte, I tell myself. That Rickerbee fella, he must o bin up to no good, tis why they was talkin bout banishment an the lyke. If you keeps yore head down an works hard, all will be well.

I listerns to the splutters o the men an the burps an farts an stinks comin from em til sleep finally swamps me.

JACK HAS A SORE HEAD WHICH PUTS HIM IN A RYTE BAD MOOD ALL DAY. Too much beer is no good for a man. When I holds the riddle out for him to shovel the coal into, his hands are unsteddy, shayke shaykin. I works as fast as I can but nothin I do is good enuff for him. He mutters an tutters under his breath as we puts the basket on the tram, all crammd full o blackest coal.

We fits a few more big peeces on top, loadin it up as much as we can fore I sets off pushin it up up up to the main rolley roads. Tis hard work, harder today for our layte nyte storyes in caban maykes me sleepy, an once or twyce I almost loses my footin. If I did Id be slip slydin back down the slope an skwish skwashd by all the coal, buryd in a hole mound o it. Some do fall, evry now an then, get broke or suffokayted or the lyke but tis the Maykers way. Part o his grand plan.

I prays again to the Mayker arfter I nearly slips. Let today not be my day, let today not be the day I joins you in the skyes. Let today be a day I ends sayfely sleepin in my bed, not a day for being skwashd or crunchd or maymd.

At the main road, I delivers the coal. Pulls the winches an pulley down, clamp clamp clamp on each fore corners an hoist hoist it up an over to the side where some uvver one will tayke it up onto the next level an so on up an up an up who knos how many more til the tip top o the mine an to the uvver side o the world.

As I emptees the basket, I think o the uvver side. O blue

34

skyes an sunshyne an the smell o grass. I kno these things eggsist. I saw em. Afore. All them years ago. But they feels so far away now. As far away an unreal as the storyes Thomas dos tell.

The last bit o coal falls out an I hoiks the basket down, loosens the clamp clamp clamps an then off I goes back down to where Jacks probly in a fowler mood than when I left him.

When I gets back, hes bin sick. Stinkin an slippy. I tells him to go back to bed an Ill cover for him but that just maykes him more cross. So I shuts my ears an eyes to him an carryes on workin. This new seam is further away from the main rolley road so each basket taykes longer to push up to it. The last seam I was doin twentee to thirtee trips a day up an back but I struggle wi fiffteen today. None o us are at our best arfter Beer Munday.

Tis a time when axidents happen. But none do today. Leest, none in this part o Bearmouth anyhows.

DEVLIN HAS STARTD JOININ US FOR OUR LETTERS. Mayker giv me payshuns. He says he can read an ryte anyways but that tis good praktiss an he can help too. I ent wantin his help so I sits as far away as I can which is not too far in trooth as spayce is tyte down here in our little dead end nook we sits in. Tobe sits ryte by him an Devlin is diffrent wi him. Softer somehow. Praps thats how the Devil gets people round to his ways, by pretendin to be nyce.

Yore letters are comin along nycely, says Thomas full o prayse for me.

Pleased, I smyles at him, a smyle that goes from my tippy tose to the top o my head. I catch Devlin lookin at me too an he smyles back soft as a kitten an I feels all upset in my stomarck lyke sick but not an I feels the heat o embarrassment flush on my fayce as I looks away.

I herd him whisperin to Thomas see as Tobe an I were layte for letters today, I herd him. Ernest, choired. Intense. An Thomas sayin, no no. Choiredly lyke. Almost under his breath but I got good hearin, better than most. I once herd a tiny beetall when it got lost an wanderd up the walls o our dorm. Bryte grene it was lyke grass on a summers day. It dint last long tho, twas gone within a day to only Mayker knos where. Still, Thomas is as calm as usual so whatever Devlin is up to, Thomas is resistin it an that maykes me feel sayfer.

I grabs Thomas the next day, as we heads to the wash at end o shifts.

Cayreful o him, I says. Cayreful o you kno who. He trubbles me Thomas an Im scared for you.

Thomas larfs at me. I can look arfter myself Newt, he says. The boys nothin to be scared o. Hes more scared hisself than he has words for. An hes lonely too. He could do wi anuvver frend. One is never enuff. He pats me on the head lyke when I was really small.

He wants me to be frends—frends wi <u>him</u>. Tis what Thomas meens. But I carnt. Not arfter I seen wi my own eyes how thawts an talk gets you into trubble wi the lykes o the shadow man. I carnt be frends wi him arfter how he mayde me feel when he smyled at me. Not arfter his talk o dayngeruss things. Revolushun an the lyke. An his nayme too. It carnt be a coincidence. Devil. In. Can it?

MAYKER SAYVE US. Hes gone. Devlin. Gone. Whisht. Lyke we all magind him in the first playce.

When I waykes up this mornin, his bed is emptee. I thawt at first he did go to the layke to wash or to piss but we normally only washs arfter shifts at nyte when we is all filthy dusty lyke from the coal. We dunt wash in the mornins. Wayste o time see. When the uvvers waykes, they goes lookin for him, shout shoutin his nayme. He ent in the mess hall for gruel. Not by the layke, not nowhere.

Jacks reportd him havin gone missin to Mister Sharp. Mr Sharp. Thomas says its spelled lyke that Mr altho only the Mayker knos why.

But hes gone. Devlin. Vanished lyke the witch up the chimnee in the story from caban. I carnt quite believe it.

Thomas thinks hes run away. Tis what he says. Maybe thats what they was whisperin about I thinks to myself.

That nyte I sneeks out when all are abed an I pads choiredly softly lyke a cat to the layke, feelin my way along the wet drip lanes an roads, over the rolley road an I slip slideys over to the layke shore. I durnt dare go in, cayse someones watchin even this layte at nyte an reports me for not payin coinage to dip myself into that cool water, but I watchs an listerns for a while. I listerns out for a body. That sound o somethin hevvy nudgin gainst the edge but there ent nothin just the lappin o water on the rocks. I dangles my fingers in an feel the white fish nibble an suck at em. Ticklin. I breethes in the cool air o the layke an lets it wash over me lyke the water dos.

We dunt get runaways here. Yore lots yore lot an theres nothin you can do about it. Rules is rules. Tis what Jack an evryone says. We works, we earn. Tis all. Sometimes really little ones cryes an bawles an so on when they starts down here. Cryes about the darkness an the heat an all, cryes thereselves to sleep but when they realize that dunt get em nowhere they stops. I kno I did. I cryed an cryed when I come here Thomas says. I carnt remember last time I cryed now.

Funny thing is I feels a bit sad bout Devlin in a way. An a bit giltee too. Maybe I got him wrong. Maybe.

Cos a Devil ent goin to run away is it?

But a boy myte.

TIME DOWN HERE IS A DIFFRENT THING SEE. Lyke on the uvver side you sees seesons chaynge, leeves grow bold an grene an fayde to gold an red, then drop off an kurl up an disappeer into sno. But Bearmouth is black. Black an warm an dark an wet an full o coal. All days all weeks all year. Forever an ever. Amen.

But tis our home see, tis our coal an our darkness an our wetness. An we is all a team. A small team what is part o a bigger team, an a bigger team an the hole mine runs lyke clokkwork wi all o us lyke little cogs. If the trapper dunt open an close his doors, the mine myte suffokayte or blow up from arfterdamp or any such things. An tis the eesiest job in the world but one o the most important. An you have to keep yore ears out all the time see. Rocks fall down so big an sharp they can cut a mans foot clene off his leg. I sees that once. Never wants to see it again an never since lyked goin down that part o the mine. Was known for falls it was an when you see a mans foot parted from him in the time it taykes to breeth in an out, you never wants to see it again an never wants to be in that sayme playce again. Not ever.

Jack has startd to coff. We all dred it down here. The coff. Hack hack hack, he goes at nyte. An the uvvers get cross. Weve all had it one time or anuvver but this is a bad un. He coffd up bits o black the uvver day at mess. Could see it in the parms o his hands lyke black slime.

There was an axident today. Two levels up. We all herd the xplosion. Felt the rumbles rippell long the walls an

40

throo our feet. Felt the rattles in our bones, in our rib cayges.

Thomas says severn were killed. Severn. I count them off on my hands, past one hole hand an onto the uvver. Theres ten beds in our dorm all crammd in, bunk beds up gainst the solid walls all faded whitewash you can scraypes off wi yore nayle. I think how I wuld feel if most o us in here were gon. Wyped out in one swoop. I counts the beds, lower bunks first. Me next to Thomas next to Tobe next to Harrisons ol bed still unfilled, then Gambles old bed at the end where Devlin was til he disappeerd. Then on the bunks above, Jack over me wi Nicholson over Thomas, Skillen over Tobe an the mewt Davidson twins who ent ever sed a word in all the time Ive known em—Will over Harrisons ol bed an Joe over Devlin. Severn men. I imagine them all wyped out in our dorm bar me an Tobe and Thomas an it maykes me feel sick to the belly.

They says it was a spark from one o the new lamps they bin tryin out on the upper levels. Two lamps they sed, an one was open at the front so the manidger sed. Jack says they only ever has one lamp tween two as they cost so much more than canduls.

But dead men carnt argyoo, says Thomas.

An all the men nod saygely.

Thomas understands xplosivs see. He manidges the openin up o seams on our level. Hes told me bout it many times, tis fayre the most dayngeruss job down a mine. You has to understand the hole feel o the rock, where the coal is headin an then playce yore dynamyte in just the ryte spot, the sweete spot he calls it. Not too much not too little an then you can opens up a new passidgeway to start diggin from. Im still thinkin about all that when Jack pipes up.

Theres talk o openin up further down in the Deep, says Jack. An he lowers his voyce ryte down. Sendin whats left o the youngs an smalls down to the deepest parts o Bearmouth. Scrapin out more o the earfs crust to send up to the uvver side. Vergin coal they calls it. Preshus stuff but small seams an hard to get at.

Jack says he wunt let me go wi out a fyte—we is a good team he an me—but he knos an I kno too that there arnt as many o us youngs here as there was. Not arfter last year when there was a huge slip slide cayve in. Well lest sed soonest mended eh. The smalls an youngs are whats needed for narrow seams an small spaces but we is also needed elsewhere in the mine too.

I dunt sleep that nyte for fear o the Deep. They says tis full o water down there. Black an sinister an evry stroke wi yore mandril splashes it all over you. They says water runs down the roadways an that yore feet are fayre soked throo. They says tis nigh on impossible to tell the coal from the stones an no man is payd to collect stones from a mine.

I wonders about Devlin too. Is he even alive? Is he wandrin one o the tunnels lost an bleatin lyke a little lamb, starvin an alone? I puts him out o my mind lyke I put the shadow man out o my mind an Rickerbee too. Ent no good thinkin about any o em. Rickerbee ent one o ours. He ent in our group who we sees in mess evryday. Hes from some uvver part o Bearmouth, some uvver mess hall an so I must needs forget about him. What the Mayker ordaynes, the Mayker maykes come troo.

JACK CAN BE A RYTE BARSTARD SOMETIMES BUT HES STILL MY HAGGER AN I AM FOND O HIM IN SOME WAYS. This morning at gruel I sees the man they calls Walsh at one o the long benches in mess. Hes the one they say was the manidger who says there was two lamps at the xplosion when we all kno that ent troo. I ent seen him before but theyve just changd his shifts round to sayme as ours an I dunt lykes the looks o him trooth be told. Hes tall wi a long narrow fayce an wild ginger hair. His fayce is. . . . Dunno. Somethin meen about it. Proper meen. Piggy lil eyes in a white doe fayce splosed wi frekkils.

He stares at Thomas lyke he ent never seen none wi darker skin afore. Praps he ent but starin is rude an Jack says that out loud. Walsh smyles at him but it ent a nyce smyle. Tis a smyle thats a warnin is what it is. We is all black under the coal dust anyways, is what Thomas says. An tis troo. Since I bin down here, weve had men from villidges so far north I ent ever herd o em. But arfter one day down here we are all dark as the nyte. The Mayker dunt cayre bout none o that anyways—if tis yore time to go, he calls you. We is only ever at his beck an call.

Thing is tho, tis best not to mayke enemees down here. A man can roowin you. They calls it an awkwud man. If you maykes trubble you becomes an awkwud man. An there is many ways o riddin yerself o an awkwud man in a mine see. A few stones added to yore tram in the dark, a playce further away from the rolley road, further to go, further to carry an lift, harder work an fewer returns. Then they labels you layzee even tho you ent an then you ent here any longer. Banishd. Thass how it works.

Best keeps an eye on that one, says Jack layter. But all o us are glad that Walsh ent tayken up Devlins old bunk or the spare in the corner.

Keep yore head down an work hard an yule be alryte. Tis what Jack always says. Rules is rules. So tis what I do. Tis what I always do.

TOBE AN THOMAS AND I (REMEMBER, SAYS THOMAS—AND TIS SPELLD AY EN DEE, DUNT FORGET THE DEE) WE ARE BACK TO WHAT WE WAS FORE DEVLIN CAYME. Tis bin (bin wi a double ee says Thomas—been) three days since he vannishd but sometimes I feels lyke I dreamt him. Dreamt that time by the layke wi his splashin and splushin and him so spinky clene and all them bruses. Dreamt him, hot heat next to me in the Maykers Hall.

But I kno I dunt dream it. Lyke I kno I dunt dream the shadow man neether.

Thomas sees I need cheerin up so he taykes me and Tobe to see the ponys on Maykers Day sted o swimmin. Arfter prayers, Thomas lytes one o his rare preshus long canduls and leads us down tunnel arfter tunnel down what feels lyke hundreds o passidges to the ponys. I smells em long fore I sees em, fore I hears em.

Stench o hot hay and hot breath and an earfy smell that is pure animal. Little ponys they are, only as high as Tobe but they is frendly enuff snuggld up in their little whitewashd staybles, chalkbords at the end wi their naymes on. Star. Mayjor. Flash. Bryte. Uvvers too. I trayce my finger across their naymes spellin em out. Tis lyke magick to be able to read and write even as little as I can.

I only gets to see the ponys once in a blue moon whenere that is but I loves em. I digs my fingers into their croppd manes and presses my fayce to them breethin in that hot musty pony smell. They whispers and whickers to each uvver in horse talk which I carnt understand but Boy who looks arfter the horses—Boy McAllister tis his nayme but evryone just calls him Boy—Boy unnerstands em. He can talk to the ponys. Whisper to em, cokes em into what he wants em to do.

Ent it crool to keep em down here? I says lyke I always do as I run my fingers throo one o the ponys manes and Boy eyes me.

No more than keepin us down here, he says chewin on a strand o hay.

Do they dreams o fields and trees and fresh grass? I says.

Boy shrugs. Ent no tellin what they dreams o. Spose we all dreams o that one day eh.

He pats Mayjor, a white dappley one wi grey circles on his back lyke someones drawn all over him. Hes my favourite is Mayjor. He snuffles up to you wi his pink velvet nose, breethes all whispry and tickly in yore ear.

I stays there as long as I can. Eekin it out, Thomas calls it, fore we have to go back. Boy dunt leeve the ponys if he can help it. Thomas says Boy prefers the ponys to people. Maybe he dos. Carnt say I blaymes him.

WE GETS TWO PROPER MEALS EVRY DAY IN MESS. Two. Tee double yoo and o lyke a round mouth. Why theres a double yoo in a word when you carnt see it or hear it I dunt rytely kno but Thomas says tis so, so it must be troo.

In the mornings we have gruel and then arfter, when we is washd and clene arfter a long day workin, we have meet and potaytoes. Boiled meet and boiled potaytoes. Tis how it is evryday. Sometimes the meet and tatties ent very hot but I lykes it better then. Tis warm Bearmouth, see, proper warm lyke and warm food just maykes a body sweat more.

I herd a tale once o three men who died aways in a single day due to lack o water cos they sweated all the moysture out o their own bodies. All o it. Imagine that. So I never eats hot food when tis really hot. Ent good for you see.

Anyways, them two meals are both in the mess hall. Long big benches, long big taybles and evryone sits wi the uvver fellas from their dorm. Tis harf full cept on Maykers Day cos o the shifts when evryone from our part o the mine is all togevver in the mess hall. Tis a twentee fore hower operayshun sayve on Maykers Day is the mine. So theres our shifts see, daytimes and the uvver ones at nyte. Or coud be the uvver way round tho givern none o us sees daylyte.

We all gets givern a peece o bred for lunch what me and Tobe eats when we goes over our letters wi Thomas. Rappd up in payper is the bred and you got to keep it clene tuckd away in yore pockit else the rats and mice steels it from you. Tobe tucks it in his pockit wi Mouse in to keep him

47

silent. I think Thomas knos about Mouse wi his sharp eyes and learnedness and all, but he ent sed nothin so maybe he dunt. Tobe keeps Mouse in a box under his bed during mess and at nytes and he ent run away since that first time. Our bred taystes stale most days but it fills the gap and tis better than nothin. I keeps myne close in my shirt pockit nyce and snug next to my little tin o matchiss for canduls.

I sees Walsh again at mess today. Flicker flicker in the lyte o the canduls reflektin back off the whitewashd walls. They keeps sayin weel have lectrick down this part o the mine in dew corse but I ent holdin my breath on that one. Parantly theres lectrick further up, beyond the Maykers Hall, but they ent worked out how to bring it this far down.

Walsh eyes me but I sees him as his eyes fall on Tobe. I dunt lyke it. I feels funny. But theres nowt I can do so I sits and eats my meets and tatties and I stays choired.

Quiet, says Thomas. Kew yoo eye ee tee. Anuvver stewpid spelling. It dunt mayke sense. But Thomas says thats how it is so it must be troo. Tis a rule, Thomas says. And rules is rules as we all knos.

TEWSDAY NYTE. We heads back to dorm arfter evenin mess and a shock awaytes us. Mayker sayve us all. Devlin is back.

His fayce is blues and blacks all down one side and swollen too. One eye puffd up so much he carnt be able to see out o it. He says nothin as he lies in his bunk.

Nothin.

Hes been returnd is all, says Jack. Runaways get brawt back. Fact that is. He says it loud so Devlin carnt help but hear.

Thomas tells me that I tryd to run away once, when I first cayme here.

I says nothin to Devlin. But I eyes him.

I never thawt Id clap eyes on him again to tell the trooth. But here he is. As real as me. Not a dream arfter all.

Im not shore if Im not a little bit pleased hes back. Just a little trooth be told.

But I also feels somethin else too. Forbodin, Thomas calls it. Tis what I feels deep inside.

A HOLE WEEK HAS GONE PAST. No, says Thomas. Whole. Double yoo haitch oh ell and ee. Whole. I carnt be standin why these double yoos, I tells him. They ent makin sense. Silent letters poppin up here and there lyke a test o a bodys payshuns. Mayker sayve me.

Anyways, a whole week has gone since Devlin was returnd and he still ent sed a word. Thomas has tryd to talk to him many a time but he just turns his head away. I offerd him a polltiss I mayde for him, a payste to help wi the brusin but he just took it in silence wi a nod o thanks but no words. The bruse on his fayce has startd to chaynge from black to blue grene. He dunt even come to letters wi us no more neether. We only sees him at meals and in dorm. He keeps hisself to hisself and he dunt even mayke eye contact.

Thomas ent givin up tho. He says to me and Tobe, you have to try, you have to keep tryin and that Devlin, or poor lad as he keeps callin him, needs soothin and simpathee.

We ent very good at those things down here. You got to be tuff to get bys down here, tuff as ol boots.

Tho I always think it should be tuff as new boots. Boots are spensive mind, but we got to pays for them out o our wayges. Sayme old. Myne are pinchin and twinchin at the tose but I durnt get anuvver pair cos o coinage costs. It ent worth it til I gets trooly desperat.

Devlin needs to tuff up, says Jack. Life o a Bearmouth boy is a hard one but tis the Maykers way. He spouts stuff lyke this at nyte sometimes when we is all abed and waytin for sleep to tayke us away.

The Mayker mayde the mines, mayde evry one o us, mayde the world, he says. The Mayker shaypes our lives, our work, our evry livin breethin moment, says Jack in his boomin voyce.

Amen, we all whisper, sayve Devlin who says nothin not a peep. Thomas blows the lyte out.

Just as Im driftin off, theres a voyce in the dark. Devlin. What about Mr Sharp?

Why by my sole, I fear the boys tung is still lodged in his head arfter all, says Jack and he larfs. Why bless me lad, what about Mr Sharp?

Who put him in charge—the Mayker? says Devlin.

Mr Sharp was poynted to his role lyke by the Master, says Jack.

And the Master. Who gayve him his role? says Devlin.

Jack ponders this. I hears him thinkin it throo in his head. Crunchin his thawts lyke pebbles. I stays silent, listernin.

Why he inherited it dunt he? The Maykers way that is.

There ent nothin but silence.

And then Devlin just says one word. Why?

Jack larfs to hisself. Why lad? Why? Well tis for the Mayker to answer that not for the lykes o us.

And Devlin says it again. Why?

Jack turns on him lyke a large rat on a small un. No larfter now, all seeriuss.

Now then lad, no thinkin o heethenish thawts in yore head. The Maykers way tis the Maykers way and tis all there is to it. All our playces are ordayned, from the smallest creeture to the graytest human mind. Tis all the Maykers grand plan ent it?

We all say amen, bar Devlin.

Why?

Such a simple word is why. I ent sed it in a long while. Not since I first cayme here when evryone asks that question. But tis been so long since we had a new lad in the dorm none o us have been askin.

I feels the uvvers fall asleep around me. Snorin and snufflin lyke old hedghogs but I carnt sleep. All I can think o is that word goin round and round lyke a spinnin coin up on one edge. Round and round. Why? Why?

I tryes and skwashes it, skwishin it flat in my thawts. I turns over in bed, turnin and turnin tryin to get comftable but my brayne wunt stop goin over and over why why til I carnt keep my eyes open no more. Why. Why. Why.

Mayker protekt me. Mayker protekt us all.

TODAY IS A BAD DAY. Im so fayre worn out that I ent as sharp as usual nor as swift neether.

Up on the rolley road when I loosen the clamps, the basket nearly falls ryte on me. Mayker preserve me. It ent that hevvy trooth be told since tis empteed an all but it gives me a fayre fryte. Maykes me kno that I ent focusin proply on the job at hand. I stands stock still for a moment just holdin my breath. And then big deep breath in, count to three and off I go back down to the pits o hell where Jack waytes.

As a rule, Jack dunt talk much whilst we work—I jokes to Tobe that he sayves it all up for meal times, lyke savin coinage. As if he has an allokayshun o words for each day and he durnt go over it. Today is diffrent tho.

That lad, he says shaykin his head whilst we loads up the basket again. That lads got to watch what he says. Dunt he realize about blasfeemin and the lyke?

He dunt wayte for a response. He never dos. Thing is, Jack says, the Mayker sets evrythin up, tis his world, the lykes o us are mayde in his image. Lyke the prayer says, he sent us down into the dark Earf to atone for the sins o our forefarvers and muvvers. And I ent seen a sine to chaynge that have you? he says, not waytin for an answer.

He gotta be cayreful, Jack carryes on. You dunt be challengin the Maykers words cos all yule get is trubble.

I sniffs to myself. Trubble is what I see in my head when I think o Devlin. Trubble and a stirrin that I ent felt the lyke o afore.

The baskets soon filld again and off I goes pushin it up and up and up all the ways to the top. My own breath fills the air around me as I puff up, push pushin til it evens out at long last.

I tryes and shut it all out. Tryes to think nothin but I carnt remember what I thawt about durin these times afore <u>he</u> cayme. Maybe I thawt about birds and grass and learnin letters but now I think o his brused fayce. Think o his question. Simple simple word but one I ent askd myself in years. Why?

Evry footstep I hear maykes it echo in my head. Why?

And his fayce is in my eyes, in my thawts I imagine the bruses gone and those coal black eyes that seem to see throo most evrythin lookin at me in my minds eye. Why is things as they are? Why is it so spensive to go back up to the uvver side? Why dos I pay so much for my boots when they dunt last me long enuff?

I tryes and stops my thawts from wandrin but tis hard to rain em in. Tis heethenish things that whirl round my head. Things are how they are, I says to myself over and over. Things are how they are. Tis how it is. Tis the rules.

But my brayne dos play tricks on me. Cos whenever I manidge to get my thawts in a lyne lyke, I hears that one word again. Why. Why.

To distrakt myself I go throo my letters, spell evry word I kno back and forth back and forth, until I tramps him out o my head. Til I push him ryte out o my thawts and back where he belongs.

I wish he ent ever come back.

TOBE AND I SITS AND WAYTES AND WAYTES FOR THOMAS BUT HE DUNT COME. So we praktisses our letters ourselves. Countin throo the alphabet lyke Thomas showd us. We dunt lyte a candul as trooth be told we are both a bit short on em so we sits there in the dark recitin lyke parrots.

A is for arfterdamp
B is for basket
C is for candul
D is for—an there he is back in my head again til I forces him out and remembers the Deep, the Deep o the Mine. D is for deep. D is for deep.
E is for eye o the pit
F is for firedamp
G is for gruel
H is for hurriers
I is for inundayshun lyke when water floods part o the mine
J is for jack roll, one o our hand winches to lift up the baskets
K is for knuk, the corner o the coalfayce
L is for lyte
M is for Mayker
N is for nyte shifts
O is for overseer lyke what Mr Sharp is
P is for pony
Q is for question when tis spelled ryte
R is for rolley road

S is for seams o coal

T is for tubs

U is for undergrawnd what we all are

V is for ventilayshun

W is for workin. And also for why which is a question I ent allowin myself to ask.

X is for xplosions tho Thomas says that ent spelled ryte but tis how I remembers it

Y is for youngs

Z is for Zebediah what is the nayme o the Master so evryone says but we ent alloud to call him that.

We says it over and over til even Tobe gets tired an cross and he dos normally have the payshuns o the Mayker hisself.

When we sees Thomas at end o shift by the pumps gettin clene I asks him where he was and he says he had bisness to attend to. That meens nothin as Thomas ent got no bisness but it meens mouth buttoned up and no tellin whilst uvvers are listernin.

But Im proved wrong on that front cos he dunt say nothin to me about it at mess, not in dorm nor for the whole next day when he turns up for letters lyke nothin ever happend. And I knos then that I has to let it go but I sees his eyes flicker over to Devlin more than once and I carnt help but wonder.

WALSH GETS INTO A FYTE WI JACK TODAY AT MESS. It happens so fast, they was at each uvvers throtes fore any o us could stop em. Thomas and Skillen pulled em off each uvver in the end and the Davidsons held the uvvers back who wantd to join in, Devlin helpin em too tho he is fayre keepin his head down since that nyte o askin why.

Walsh see, he ent a popyoular man, hes a bully and theres plenty o uvvers who wunt mind a pop at him and all. But Will and Joe, the Davidsons see, they are fayre as fayre as Jack says and they ent wantin all out fytin in the mess speshully cos not evryone had eaten yet and we ent never havin enuff food to wayste none o it.

Walshs nose was bleedin crimson and he was glarin ryte at Jack as if he could murder him just by lookin. Jack is grinnin at him pleased as punch as he come off better out o it but Walshs look is dirty lyke and I wuldunt dares be on the wrong side o him I swear it.

Better watch yore back from now on Coombes, says Walsh throo gritted teeth and Jack larfs at him.

Watch yore own self, Walshie, he says. You ent a popyoular man down here you ent so if anyone needs to keep eyes and ears clene and peeld for trubble its yore self man. Jack larfs again. Ive had better fytes from young Tobe here than Ive had from you.

Walshs eyes flicker over me and Thomas to Tobe and back to Jack. Hes taykin us in, rememberin us out o all the men in the mess. Rememberin our fayces. Thomas pulls me closer to him never lettin his eyes off Walsh.

It ent our fyte but it seems lyke we all mayde an enemee today.

JACK SAYS HE WAS DEFENDIN US. That Walsh had been eyin me up o all people sayin what a pritty young thing I was and smirkin in that way he has. I ent shore if Jacks tellin the trooth as sometimes he is one to tell a tall tale. But neverless I listerns to Thomas layters on the way back to dorm when he says steer cleer o Walsh.

I had been doin, I says, but it ent my fawlt they got into a fyte.

Thomas nods but he taykes his hand then and holds it on my fayce on one side, gentle lyke. You are a preshus thing, he says. You are a preshus thing Newt, lyke my own chylde. He smyles and his fayce lytes up. He ent ever calld me that afore now.

Lyke his own chylde. I hold those words close to me as if theyll protekt me from all things bad.

I dunt kno what to say back to him so I just smyles and pats his hand insted. As we heads back to dorm, I feel an arm on my sholder and tis Devlin, he nods at me and tis the first time in an ayge he has lookd at me strayte in the fayce. I nod back and he lets go and heads back to dorm ahead o me and I ent shore rytely what to think.

THOMAS MISSES OUR LETTERS AGAIN TODAY. Despyte all that stuff about bein lyke his own chylde he cleerly ent that interested in keepin myne and Tobes educayshun goin proper.

I ent seen him and Devlin talkin direktly but Im certain tis where he is and Im cross too. Hes our frend. Ours. Me and Tobe have known him for years whilst Devlin ent been here more than a month all added up.

And Im worryd too. Worryd about Thomas—what happend to those men that was found in the layke that time. What happend to that Rickerbee bein beaten and banishd. If Thomas and Devlin are up to somethin they could end up lyke that an all.

At end o shift at wash time, we strips down to nothinness by the pumps and I keeps my eyes out but Thomas ent there. Devlin is deep in the kayoss o bodies comin off shift. But then I sees him. Walsh.

Eyein me up as he suds hisself down. Theres a tattoo over his back, black as coal, curve o a wolfs fayce lookin back at me. Walsh smyles at me so I look elsewhere an mayke shore Tobes fayce is clene for mess. Jack smacks Walsh on the back lyke theyre the best o frends now but they ent and Walsh has that look in his eye lyke a hungree dog thatll tayke yore arm off in a single bite.

THOMAS DUNT SHOW UP TIL MESS HAS STARTD. He dos have a haunted look about him. Lyke the wayte o all Bearmouth is on his sholders. When he taykes his playce on our bench, he glances at Devlin and I sees him shayke his head a little.

Where you been all day? I says. Me and Tobe missd you at letters.

I was uvverwyse occupyed, he says. Sorry to you both but it carnt be helped.

Where was you then? says Tobe and Thomas smyles.

Tryin to do the impossible, he says.

Jack eavesdrops see and he sticks his beek in. What you been doin Thomas? he says grinnin. Tryin to get rid o our new frend Walshy eh?

Thomas shaykes his head. Now ent a playce for tellin, he says. Wayte til dorm and Ill tell all.

Jack is as intreegd as the rest o us so we eats up greedily and fast lyke so we can get back.

Thomas checks nowun else is behind us as we heads into dorm and then heeves the wooden panel in playce that we use as a door on rare occayshuns to keep the drafts out when tis blowin up a gayle around the tunnels.

Jack rubs his hands lyke Thomas is goin to tell him the best story he dun ever hear but Thomas maykes us all sit first. He lytes a candul and playces it on the floor so we can all sees each uvver. Our shadows flicker round us on the whitewashd walls.

I askd for more coinage for us all, he says and I see him

glance at Devlin when he says it. I asked for more coinage cos I see all o us are hungree men. And I see that all o us have boots that dunt fit too well.

I feels him lookin at myne and then he carryes on.

I askd Mr Sharp for a payrise for us all and he sed it werent his bisness to be able to agree such a thing an that Id have to see Mr Johnson.

Jack larfs at this poynt. You dunt do it, did ya Thomas lad? See the Master hisself, did you? Boys got balls o steel to be askin Mr Sharp for anythin, surprised he dunt just cuff you round the fayce.

Thomas cleers his throte. I askd very nycely, he says.

Nyce dunt get you nowhere in this world, snorts Jack. Do it lads?

Skillen snorts too as dos Nicholson but the Davidsons stay quiet as mice.

But nyce got me a meetin wi the Master, says Thomas and we all goes silent again.

The lytes in Mr Sharps office where we met, they did hurt mine eyes they were so bryte. But I can confirm that the Master is a tall man, says Thomas, lyke they say he is. Taller than any o us and he wears a tall hat as high as his head again.

We bends in and listerns xtra cayreful now as none o us has ever seen the Master, hes lyke a mythikal creeture. Lyke a unikorn or a gryffyn.

But he is a man mayde o sturn stuff, says Thomas. And he thinks we are all payd well enuff for what we do.

Jack snorts. Tis the Maykers will to pay us this amount. Tis always been the sayme Thomas, haggers been payd sixtee since long afore I come to Bearmouth. Sayme rayte sayme job wi a bonuss for xtra haulin, thass how it is.

Why? I hear a voyce say and am startld to find it cayme from within me.

Cos thats how it is Newt, says Jack softly. Tis just how it is. How tis always been, how twill always be. Things is as they is.

But in the Maykers Prayer it says he will send a sine, I find myself sayin. How will we kno when we see it?

Jack reetches out and rubs my head lyke Im fore or fyve years old. Bless ya Newt, he says, tis not for youngs to consern their selfs over. It ent happenin in our lifetimes tis for shore.

I stays silent but my eyes drift to Devlin and he looks back at me for a moment, those coal black eyes borin down at me.

Our boots are threads, our clothes fall apart, our canduls are rasshund and yet we work our soles away six days out o severn, says Thomas. Wi out us Bearmouth cannot funkshun and yet I ask are we properlee rekompenced?

He leeves it hangin in the air.

I feels my heart beatin in my chest lyke tis goin to burst out, lyke that time I cawt Tobes Mouse and held it close in my hands. Flutter flutter flutter went its little heart til I let it go and gayve it back to Tobe. Here tis. Tis the trubble I was fearin. This is it comin lyke an out o control truck on a rolley road hurtlin hurtlin.

Tis how its always been Thomas, says Jack cayrefullee and slow lyke. I got more years on you and tis how its always been since ever I can remember.

I chews my lips. Ent ryte tho is it? And again I am fayre startld to find it cayme from within me.

Devlin interrupts sudden lyke. Newt spekes trooth. Tis not ryte that we dunt uok these things. This playce is more lyke hell than anywhere I have ever been and yet we do not ask why we are treeted no better than animals.

Thomas jumps in. Where are the sayfety lamps that we were promisd? Why do we pay so much for canduls and clothes when we cannot do our job wi out them?

Have a cayre Thomas, says Jack sharp lyke. This lad here, hes been puttin ideas in yore head from the uvver side. I kno yore a learned man but still. It dunt do well to question the Maykers way.

Tis not the Maykers way, says Devlin. Tis Mr Johnsons way.

I can feel my world crumblin around me and I reetch out my hand and grab Tobes and hold it tyte as I can. I feel his hand tremblin in mine.

Well you ent convincin me is all, says Jack arfter a long silence.

I dunt ask you to, says Thomas. But just think on what Ive sed is all. Think on it as you work yoreself til you are fayre so tired you can barely keep yore eyes open. Til yore boots are worn thin. Sayme goes for all o you, he says lookin round the dorm, eyes on Nicholson and Skillen, eyes on Will and Joe, eyes on me and Tobe lingerin lyke fore he turns to Devlin. Tis all I ask, says Thomas. Carnt say fayrer than that eh.

And wi that he blows out the candul.

TIS MAYKERS DAY THE VERY NEXT DAY AND I FEEL IT AROUND ME PRICKLIN LYKE HEAT. The swell o thinkin things preeveeus unthawt o. Heethenish thawts. Dayngeruss thawts. Tis as if we have opend a box not ment for us and none o us wants to admit it.

The day passes in a blur. Thomas is distant wi us all day and Devlin is silent. Jack sings xtra loud at prayer. I hear him bellow in my ear. I mouth the words quietly singin lyke I always do but my heart ent in it. My hands, my arms, they lift and pray, my maw opens and closes as I sing but my head is elsewhere, think thinkin.

The men go to caban and Thomas leeves us.

I want to be on my own for a short while, he says, forgive me. And then he is gone.

I go down to the layke wi Devlin and Tobe but I dunt go in, I sits at the edge hearin em splosh around and I feel sick. Somethin is diffrent. Tis just a Maykers Day lyke any uvver I tells myself over and over. But it ent.

Devlin pulls himself out o the water and sits close by me. I feels the heat from him lyke a cloud. I want to reetch out and touch him but I durnt.

I wunt bite, he says. You kno you can always talk to me, he says. We have more in common than you think.

But I dunt say nothin.

Thank you for the polltiss, he says. When I cayme back and the bruses were bad, I think it helpd.

I dunt rytely kno what to say to him so I just nods. We

65

sits in silence for a bit and arfter a while he gives up and goes back in the layke.

What have you dun? I thinks to myself hearin him splash in the water and tease Tobe. What have you startd?

And I feel lyke I dunt kno nothin no more.

NEXT MORNIN TIS BACK TO WORK AND JACK DUNT SAY NOTHIN TO ME ALL DAY. Just hacks and hacks at the coalfayce but he dos it wi a speed and a fury I ent seen for a long time. Tis lyke Maykers Day has fired him up somehow.

The rhythm o workin is good for a brayne see. Repeat repeat, yore hands and legs, yore whole body workin as one and yet yore brayne wandrin off in all sorts o direkshuns and wi nowun to stop it. Tis useful for learnin letters and goin over things lyke spellin in yore head. Tis not useful when you is tryin to not think o uvver things.

Thinkin is dayngeruss, says Jack to me once. A long time ago that was. But I ent ever forgot it. But I allowes my mind to wander, I let it spread and shift lyke ink spillin on payper.

Why is it so spensive for us to use the lift sharft to travel back up to the uvver side when the lift must in trooth go up and down all the time to tayke the coal out? Why is it we got to pay for the very kwipment we need to work on top o all else?

I rap my own nuckles. It ent no good thinkin things lyke this Newt, I says to myself. Tis a slippry slope. Thomas is a gifted wordsmyth and a learned man to boot and if he carnt be convincin the lykes o the Master for a payrise or nothin no body can.

But it keeps creepin back in my head, creep creep lyke a spyder that wunt go aways no matter how much you tryes to get rid o it. And I thinks bout the coinage I earns and how much Jack earns and yet I works as hard as him and still all o us livin on top o each uvver wurse than Boys ponys.

I pushs it to the back o my brayne and I hum songs to myself in its sted. Songs from Maykers Day and uvvers too. Sometimes at caban the men do sing uvver songs—we hears them sometimes at letters faynte off in the distance. I dunt kno all the words but I knos some o the chewns so I hums them insted to keep my brayne from wandrin. I goes over my letters too, hummin to myself workin out how to spell words I can say but cannot yet write down.

At the top o the rolley road, anuvver fella is there when I arrives. I hears em knokkin about in the dark.

Hello, I says. Cos there ent never normally anyone up here at the sayme time as me.

Hello, I says again but nobody answers me. I dunt lyke it. Tis straynge. People always talks to each uvver when they bumps into a fella body down the mine.

I can hear you, I says tryin to sound confeedent lyke.

I can hear you.

The footsteps shuffles off into the distance and a shiver goes down my neck. I think o the man in the shadows that time. I cast my mind back tryin to remember his voyce but the fear o runnin away has near wrote over it. I put it to the back o my mind and carryes on. For what else can a body do?

AT MESS AT THE END O OUR SHIFT, A DREDFUL THING DOS HAPPEN. I am all adrift lyke a boat lost at see.

Tobe has gone. Tayken by Walsh.

We sits at mess lyke we always dos, eatin our meet and tatties when Mr Sharp comes over to us, bisness lyke, and poynts at Tobe.

He looks over at Walsh.

This one? he says and Walsh nods, smyle growin on his fayce lyke a bloom o algee. Up you get, says Mr Sharp and Tobe gets to his feet, fayce all confewsed as are we all. Walsh is down a boy, says Mr Sharp, and they is venturin down the Deep for a new seam. They needs a small young to go wi them. Mr Sharp looks at me at this poynt for a while.

I stand and step forwud wi my arms crossd. What bout me then? I says. I ent much bigger.

Walsh larfs and it ent a nyce larf neether. Oh no, he says, starin at me. Not you. Not yet anyways.

Mr Sharp shaykes his head at me. You ent the sayme size, he says. This lads much smaller than you. Hell do.

Tobe stands there, not knowin what to do. He ent a boy o much words so I say somethin for him.

He carnt do this, can he? I says to Thomas. On what awthoritee?

On the Masters, says Thomas.

Thats ryte, says Mr Sharp. I act as his voyce here. Tis what it is.

Skillen stands up and shaykes his head. The boy is milne,

he says. We are a team me and Tobe and I say you carnt tayke my trayler aways wi out my says so.

Mr Sharp shaykes his head. Mr Johnson says the Deep has got vergin coal that needs to be got out and the small youngs are to work on that as a matter o pryoritee.

You goin ta replayce him then? says Skillen. Eh?

Mr Sharp shaykes his head. It wunt be for long, just a week or so and yule have to be hagger an trayler in the meentime but thats how it is.

I ent an awkwud man, says Skillen firmly lyke. I ent an awkwud man and you be treatin both me and Tobe lyke I am.

Mr Sharp shaykes his head again. Yule be fully rekompenced, he says. We will pay twyce over for the lone o this one for a week.

Skillen dunt lyke it that much is cleer but there ent no argyooin wi Mr Sharp. The overseer is the iron rule see and what he says goes.

Tobe stands there, not knowin what to say or do.

Mr Sharp slaps him on the back hard and maykes him stumble. Eat yer meets lad, he says. Then when yore dun, off you go and sit wi Walsh. You starts tomorro. And wi that Mr Sharp is off somewhere else leavin us to dygest his words.

Walsh smyles at Tobe. I wunt bite lad, he says lookin xactly lyke he wuld. Just lyke that wolf drawn on his back.

Tobe dunt want no more supper tho. He sits there in silence. And trooth be told all our appertytes are gone to dust.

I dunt really have to go do I? he says sudden lyke.

Skillen pats him on the sholder. It ent for long son, he says. Yule be back amongst us all afore you knos it. Ent that ryte?

70

The Mayker will be wi you, says Thomas. The Mayker is always wi you Tobe.

We nod and mutter but still, I dunt lyke it.

I dunt want to go, says Tobe in a crackd voyce and I remembers then how young he is.

Skillen smyles at him, come on Tobe lad, it ent for long.

Jack gets up from the bench and goes over to Walsh, hands out lyke he ent got nothin to hide.

Walsh, he says, cleerin his throte. Any harm comes to that boy and—

Walsh plays wi his nyfe from dinner, turnin it over in his hands. Wunt be no harm dun to him, he says interruptin Jack. We will treet him fayrely wunt we lads?

And Walshs team nod there heads.

Mayke shore thats the cayse then, says Jack.

Corse axidents do happen sometimes dunt they? says Walsh. And ent nowun to blayme for an axident eh?

Jack glares at him. Any harm and yule have me to answer to. That cleer? says Jack.

Me too, says Thomas.

And me, growls Skillen.

Walsh grins at us and shrugs. Corse. Corse.

Tobe is tremblin when he stands up. He comes over to me and gives me a hug. Will you look arfter Mouse for me? he says in my ear.

I nod. Corse, I whispers.

Keep him sayfe in the dorm til Im back, he says.

Corse, I says.

He holds my hand tyte and hugs me again. Will you say bye to Mouse for me and all? whispers Tobe.

I nods. But shore as shore yule be back in no time eh, I says.

Tobe nods, he lets go o me afore walkin over to Devlin and huggin first Thomas and then Devlin. Devlin looks at me over Tobes sholder and tis a straynge matter but I carnt read his fayce.

Come on lad, growls Walsh and Tobe lets go o Devlin and walks over to Walsh. One step at a time, hangin back lyke, lookin down at the floor.

Can I stay in the sayme dorm as them? he says noddin back at us lot and Walsh shaykes his head.

No lad. Yore part o my team now and what I says, you dos. And I says yore in my team, you stay in my dorm wi my lads, he says. Startin from now.

Skillen smyles at Tobe, forcin it out. Tis only a week lad, severn days hence and yule be back in yer own bed sayfe as you lyke eh. We will sees you arfter shift here in mess and at wash time an all. It ent lyke we disappeerd or nothin is it lad? One week is all. And we will sees ya tomorro wunt we?

Tobe nods his head.

Walsh indicaytes a spayce next to him and Tobe goes and sits down next to him.

I dunt lyke this, I mutters under my breath. I dunt lyke this at all.

Tis the Maykers way, says Jack. Tis all.

Thomas puts a hand on my sholder and I see Devlins jaw set tyte as stone.

It ent ryte, I say. It ent bloody well ryte.

THE BED NEXT TO ME IN THE DORM IS EMPTEE. Tobes bed.
The silence comin from it maykes me fayre want to screem
but there ent no poynt. I kno Ill see him tomorro at mess
but it ent the sayme.

It ent the bloody sayme.

Skillen ent sayin nothin but on the way back arfter mess
I felt a hand reetch out to me and when I lookd back it was
Devlin. His hand brushd myne lytely as if he was wantin to
hold it and I felt the heat go ryte up my arm as I took my
hand away. Just for one breef moment I felt better but now
I feels sick just thinkin bout poor Tobe wi none to stand up
for him.

I check on Mouse at nyte when all are abed but the
bugger dos bite me when I tryes to tayke him out o his box.
I drops him for a moment and he skurrys under my bed but
by the mornin he has fayre disappeerd.

Tis anuvver bad nyte when I carnt manidge to sleep
proper neether.

Mouse will come back, I promisses myself. Mouse will
come back. I ent lettin Tobe down, they will both come back
and all will be well. I says it over and over.

But that ent all thats bovverin me. Too many thawts in
my head it is. Heethenish thawts. Heethenish things I dunt
ryte kno the answer to. And I think back to what Devlin did
say when he first cayme—it taykes one person.

Can that be ryte? I asks myself. Just one? And I dunt
rytely kno the answer.

73

TOBE DUNT MAYKE EYE CONTACT THE NEXT MORNIN AT MESS.
He looks well enuff but he ent lookin this way thats for shore.

Skillen shouts out to him. Alryte there Tobe lad, and Tobe nods wi out lookin up.

Walsh puts his hand on him lyke a clamp and Tobe glances up for a second fore lookin back down.

If you ent alryte lad, you kno where to come, says Skillen in a loud voyce.

Tobe nods.

Evrythins fine, says Walsh all calm lyke. Nyce lad by all akkounts.

I thinks about Tobe the rest o the day, wondrin what tis really lyke to be down in the Deep, whevver tis as wet and horriball as they all say. Bein glad that I ent down there but worryin about Tobe all the sayme. Worryin about Mouse too, how Im goin to tell Tobe that I wunt troo to my word. That Mouse has gone.

There ent nothin you can do, I keeps sayin to myself. There ent nothin you can do about Tobe. I am just a young and I dunt have a voyce. What wuld I says anyways? It ent ryte you taykin him away lyke that? Who wuld listern to me? Who wuld listern to a young?

I think o what Thomas sed the uvver nyte. The boots, the canduls, they is all our propertee but then, in our own ryte, ent we just the propertee o Mr Sharp, o the Master to do whatever he wishes eh? Ent that all we are? Tools for a job thats all. Lyke Boys ponys.

ARFTER SHIFT THERE ENT NO SINE O WALSH OR HIS TEAM AT THE PUMPS. Plenty o uvver men there from uvver dorms but I keeps my eyes peeld and they ent there. We all notiss it.

It ent til harfway throo mess that we sees em come in, hair slickd wet from their wash. Tobes fayce red and raw as tho hes been scrubbed ryte clene.

I stands up and goes strayte over to em. Tobe, whats it lyke then, the Deep eh?

He dunt look up. Warm and wet lyke they says, he says in a teeny voyce.

But yore alryte tho, I says, and he nods wi out lookin up still. Well as long as yore alryte, I says and he nods.

And Mouse? he says.

Mouse is fine, I says, lyin throo my teeth. Hes in his box and sayfe as ever. And you, you alryte really? I says and Tobe nods.

But I ent shore he is alryte. Dunt forgets yore letters, I says and he nods again. The alphabet and all that, I says. Be seein ya tomorro then Tobe, eh, I says and he nods.

But he ent ryte. He ent spekin freely is what Im thinkin. But theres only six more days to go and then hes back wi us where he belongs in our dorm.

On the wall near my bed, Ive scritch scratched severn little lynes to mark the days that Tobe ent here. Today I scratch one throo wi my nayle. One down. Still no sine o Mouse but praps hell come back when Tobe dos.

Tis troo that there are uvver youngs down here too but

75

we dunt see em cept a handful at mess or on Maykers Day. Mixin ent enkurridged see. Gatherin is forebidden outside o mess, caban and dorms. Tis the way its always been. Rules is rules. Tobe was the only uvver young in our dorm fore Devlin cayme but Devlin is an older young so he dunt count I figurs.

I smyles to myself when I think o Tobe comin back. We been learnin our letters together me and Tobe ever since he cayme here and we helps each uvver out. Hes a smart lad is Tobe. I think o what Thomas says to me that time about bein lyke his own chylde and I realize thats how I think o Tobe, lyke hes my own bruvver.

I hope he will forgive me for losin Mouse but you carnt keep a wild creeture in captivitee if it dunt want to be there. Can you?

THAT NYTE I CARNT HELP BUT THINK O HOME. Mayker
forgive me.

Home. I ent thawt about that word for ever such a long
time. Bearmouth is my home now. I tryes and thinks back
to how it was when I was on the uvver side, but I struggles to
see it cleerly now.

I wonder if Ma even remembers me. Wonder if theres
yet anuvver baby at home that I ent knowin about. Thing is,
Ma always sed shed write but she never has since that first
time. But I writes to her, Thomas helpd me fore I knew my
letters better but I writes evry six months I do and I ent herd
nothin back since she confirmd she was gettin the coinage
I was sendin. I harden my heart to it cos I kno it costs to
send post an all and I ent able to send her as much as Id
lyke.

Thomas ent got any famly to speke o so he dunt have
anyone to write to. I do wonder tho if Ma still thinks o me.
I spect she dos evry time the coinage arryves but I wonders if
she still remembers.

You was but a myte when you cayme here, says
Thomas and trooth be told I carnt remember much afore
Bearmouth. I remember sounds tho, birds singin and
the breeze in the trees and things lyke that. Cows mooin
from the big farm and the trit trot o horses hoovs. And
I remember feelins too. Lyke the warmth o the sun on yer
fayce and closin yore eyes to the sheer pleshure o it. And the
coldness o the pond at the big farm if you even so much as

77

dipped a toe in and the sheer shock that went ryte throo you and mayde you jump and larf and skweel lyke a piggy all at the sayme time. And I remember bein crushd in a room all o us all piled in, me and Ma and Auntie Soo who ent really my aunt and all the cuzzins an all. And next door the uvver room which needed keepin cleer for any o the men who did come in. And feelin hungree so hungree but tryin not to eat much as all o us are in the sayme boat, as Ma says. One o my bestest memorees is the sensayshun o feelin spinky clene arfter a barth in the shayred kitchin. A rare occurents but oh such pleshure. There ent no barths at Bearmouth. Just the pumps arfter shift at the waterfall and swimmin in the layke but the layke ent as warm lyke a barth is. What I wuldnt giv for a barth. Oh Id pay coinage for that I wuld. Big coinage an all.

I dunt dream o any o that tho. I dream o someone tryin to hold my head under the water and I waykes up gaspin as tho Im fayre drownin in the layke.

When I come to, proper lyke, I looks at the lynes I scratchd in the wall and I cross off anuvver wi whats left o my nayles.

IN THE MORNIN WHEN WE GETS DRESSED DEVLIN ASKS ME IF IM ALRYTE AND I NOD AND SHRUG AND SAY O CORSE.

But I also want to shayke him and screem in his fayce. All this cos o you. Thomas talkin things we ent ever dared afore. My brayne all mixd fayre up wi dayngeruss thawts, Tobe tayken by Walsh, his belovd Mouse lost and all cos o you. But I dunt do it. Trooth be told, I ent shore it is all his fawlt but it feels lyke it. Mayker forgive me.

Fore he cayme, Devlin, I dunt mind gettin chaynged in front o evryone but now I feels his eyes on me and I turns away, dressin wi my back to him. I keeps my unders on lyke always but I looks the uvver way.

I asks Thomas once, when will I have the sayme as the men, the sossagemeet that hangs tween their legs? And Thomas says myne will grow in dew time but it ent showin any sine o growin. Maybe tis cos Im not one thing or tuvver that meens I ent got one yet.

I notissd ayges ago too that when the men piss they do so throo their sossagemeet but I must needs skwat lyke a dog to piss. Jack sed it ent harf funny watchin me do that when he cayme across me taykin a piss down the tunnels but hes got fayre used to it now.

I thinks about Thomass storyes and the witches house and me and Devlin and Tobe livin there in a house in the woods happy ever arfter and I thinks to myself how sad that there ent no house in the woods and there ent no happy ever arfter. And then I starts thinkin about that little word again—why. Why ent there no happy ever arfter?

I clamps down on it in my head. Clamp clamp lyke on the basket. Shushin it away. It dunt do to question such things, Jack says. Things is as things is.

But it feels lyke that little bit o red ember on a fire that wunt quite go out. It stays there flickrin at the back o my head.

Tobe wunt mayke eye contact at gruel and he dunt even finish his bowl.

Fyve more days I thinks to myself. Just fyve more arfter today and then he is back wi us. Home where Tobe belongs.

THERES AN AYKE IN MY BELLY THE LYKES O WHICH I ENT FELT AFORE. It feels lyke someone has punched me ryte below the belly button. I double over wi cramps harfways up the main rolley road and I feels sick wi it too. It taykes all my strength to not let the basket slip back down and tayke me wi it.

Arfter I emptees the basket out at the top, I gags and retchs lyke Im to be sick but nothin comes out. It passes arfter a while and I gets back to work but it bovvers me all day. I want to ask Thomas about it as I ent gettin no sympathee from Jack I knos that for shore.

I dunt get a chance to talk to Thomas tho cos at letters Devlin is there and I carnt ask Thomas in front o him so I focus on spellin quiet insted. Tis a funny way o spellin things but Im awfull glad Thomas is such a good teecher else it ent maykin sense to any man or boy. Engerlish is a straynge langwidge to be shore.

Thomas says my vokabullairee is comin along very nycely and Devlin says tis good to hear me talk so much cos he first thawt I was almost mewt lyke Will and Joe I was so quiet.

I eats my crust o bred and bask in their prayse lyke it were the best mornin sun wi all the promiss o a perfekt day but I misses Tobe somethin dredful. It ent lyke we is competittiv see but we sort o are a bit. I got more years on him but hes bryte, so between us I thinks we learns faster cos o pushin each uvver on.

Devlin sees me thinkin and smyles at me. He ent harf

handsum when he smyles, the candul lyte flicker flickrin over his cheeks dusted black wi coal dust.

It ent long Newt, he says. Tobe will be back in no time. And I nod.

But hes wrong there see. Hes wrong. Cos disarster is a comin.

AT MESS, TOBES FAYCE IS BLUE ALL ROUND HIS LEFT EYE LYKE SOMEONE PUNCHD HIM STRAYTE IN THE FAYCE.

An axident, says Walsh as he looks over to our bench and he shrugs ryely. Easy dun, says Walsh.

Tobe, says Skillen warily lyke, was it an axident?

And Tobe nods his head still wi out maykin eye contact. You could cut the air wi a nyfe so you could but Jack and Skillen dunt want to push it cos it myte mayke things worse still for Tobe so we all just sits there, appertytes waynin away as the meet goes cold on our plates and us all knowin our hands are tyed behind our backs.

That nyte the cramps return again and I lays in bed doubled ryte over tryin my best not to mayke a sound.

If Tobe were here, Id reetch out to him and maybe even sneek into his bed for warmth and a hug and a fuss wi Mouse if he dunt bite me but he ent here, neether o em are. I ent seen Mouse since he ran off that first nyte Tobe wunt here.

I carnt affords to be sick neether cos sickness meens no coinage and no coinage meens bein mayde into debt. If yore sick see you carnt work but you still got yore boots and canduls and food and all else to pay for. And even for a day you start losin coinage and if yore proper sick, soon the mine owns evry peece o you and you got to pays it back see, bit by bit, fore yore earnin again which meens no coinage to send home for the lykes o me to my Ma and no beer for the lykes o the men

I goes over and over it in my head, carnt be sick, just yore maginayshun is all.

When I feel a hand on myne I nearly screems the playce down. Tis Devlin.

You alryte? he says whisperin.

I nod.

Shore? he says and I whispers back.

Yes, shore.

Sorry if I wayked you, he says.

You dunt wayke me, I says.

Alryte, he says.

And I hear him pad back to bed.

Tis only when I wype my fayce that I realize I been cryin.

IN THE MORNIN AT GRUEL THERE ENT NO SINE O TOBE AT ALL.
Just an emptee playce next to Walsh. Walsh says he must o
run off but that ent the sort o thing Tobe wuld do.

Skillen is worryd and we finishes gruel as fast we can
so as to try and find Tobe. He ent back in the dorm and we
looks for him down at the layke and in caban and in the
old dead end where we praktisses letters but he ent in any o
those playces. We carnt afford to look for him all day so we
heads to work but that sinkin feelin is there in me and I ent
shore if its the cramps or somethin else. But it dunt bode
well is what Im thinkin.

IM THE ONE WHO FINDS HIM.

Arfter shift when we all heads to the pumps to wash ourselves, Tobe still ent nowhere to be seen tho Walshs men are all there rubbin thereselves clene.

I was hopin and hopin hed just turn up lyke it were all a joke or somethin.

But when we turns the pumps off and are all dryin off I hears a sound bobbin at the edge o the layke.

I kno afore I sees it that tis him. I kno the moment I hears that sound.

Thomas is about to blow out the last canduls when I shouts out to him. I tryes to shout as loud as I can but my voyce has gone all dry and I suddenlee ent got as many words as I thawt I had.

I go on my nees, still just in my unders and I reetches out to the water. Thomas comes over holdin the candul in his hand, the pool o lyte around him lyke a haylo.

I kno its him.

He ent no wayte at all even in death. Lyte as a fether despyte the waterloggd clothes. I tryes to pull him out and Devlin runs to help. Together we hoyks him out and sits and looks at him, body fayce down on the wet black rocks.

I sobs out a big sound that echos round the layke cavern and I feel the uvvers gather around me in the lyte. Skillen and Jack. Will and Joe.

Thomas leans forwud and gentlee gentlee turns him over.

Tobe.

His fayce is swollen a bit wi the water but there ent no mistaykin him.

A rayge fills me up so strong that Im a runnin towards Walsh fore anyone can even think to stop me. I screem and beat and beat him til he grabs both my arms and holds em up high so I carnt hit him no more.

Learn yore playce, he says and throws my arms down and slaps me hard round the fayce. And I kno then that I wuld kill him—if I had a nyfe on me Id alreddy have stabbd him wi it, Mayker forgive me so I wuld.

Im breethin so hard and fast I want to tayke all my fury and throw it in his fayce but I feel Devlins hand pon my sholder holdin me back and the fyte goes out o me lyke a candul blown out.

Here Coombes, says Walsh, call yore pups off. I ent got no beef wi them.

Jack now looks lyke a mountin all rock and hard and he goes strayte up to Walsh and throws a punch ryte in his mouth. Walsh goes to hit back but Jacks too fast for him and he punches him again and again. Walshs men watch but they ent joynin in. They ent got the fyte for this.

Jack knoks Walsh to the ground and hits him again til Skillen and the Davidsons drag him off.

Axident wunt it? says Walsh, wypin his blooded fayce. Axident, musta been else the lad drownd hisself on purpos and we kno seweesyde is a sin ent it cos the Mayker tells us so.

Thomas is still croutchd by Tobe and when he stands up and turns round, candul still in his hand, he poynts a finger towards Walsh lyin on the ground.

Why dos the boy have marks round his neck? he says wi a

voyce terriball lyke thunder that I ent ever herd come out o his mouth afore.

Axident, musta been, says Walsh wi narrowd eyes.

What axident can cawse a lad to have marks round his neck that look so much lyke a liggatchur? says Thomas barely containin his anger.

Walsh shrugs. Boy maybe tryd to hang hisself and drownd in its sted praps, he says. Why not get Mr Sharp down here and see what he thinks eh?

There is silence in the cavern now. All eyes are on Thomas. See Mr Sharp, if theres trubble in the mine anywhere, he charges coinage to come and sort it out and he dos charge that coinage back to the man who he deems to be at fawlt. And we all kno that ent goin to be Walsh.

Walsh stands up, brushin hisself down lyke he just fell over and he swaggers over to us.

Youngs lyke this—he poynts at me—they die down here all the time, he says. Drownd or crushd or gassd or somethin. You thinks you can pin this on me? he says wi a lopsided gryn. Good luck wi that, he says. Cos I dunt think Mr Sharp will tayke yore word gainst myne will he?

And Thomas, who I ent ever seen tayke a pop at a man in the whole time I kno him, he swings back and he knoks Walsh clene down wi one fist.

Walsh hisses as he wypes his fayce, sittin back on his nees.

This meens war you kno, he spits voyce red wi blood. This meens bloody war. And he looks at me and poynts. That ones next, he says. That ones next for the Deep.

And Thomas kicks him ryte on the side o his head. Kicks him.

If you come for Newt, Mayker help me Ill knok yore

head off yore body so fast you wunt never see it comin, he says.

Is that a threat? says Walsh. Sounds lyke a threat to me.

This meens war is what you says, Jack spekes up. And theres only one o you.

Joe and Will step up behind him. Skillen appears too, carryin Tobe in his arms and lookin as if he myte crye at any moment.

Theres only one o you, says Jack. And theres six o us. Severn if you inclood Newt and tis a handy lad wi his fists eh?

Walsh stands up and his men stay a step or two away from him.

But I got ryte on my side, he says. And more important than that I got Mr Sharp on my side see. And he smyles even as the blood drip drops from the end o his nose.

And I kno then that this dunt end here. Today wi Tobe being killd. This ent the end—this is only the start. And that sayme nyte, when Thomas slips me a nyfe he steels from mess, I kno that things ent gonna get better any time soon.

WE DUNT BURY BODIES DOWN HERE IN THE MINE AS TIS A WORKIN ENVYROMENT SEE. Arfter we says prayers over Tobe, we brings his body back to the dorm and rolls him up in the sheet from his bed. Tuck him up nyce and neet lyke.

I feel hevvy evrywhere lyke somethin pressin down on all o me but none o us speke. It feels wrong to brayke the silence as we gentlee wraps him up lyke a babe in a cot.

We says our goodbyes to him taykin it in turn to whisper in his ear. Tis hard to say farewell to Tobe cos we all kno we are his only famly. He ent got none on the uvver side see—sent down here as an orfan. I kiss him on his forehead and tis cold as anythin. It dunt even look lyke him no more. This shell o a lad in front o me. It dunt look lyke Tobe at all. Hes alreddy gone to be united wi the Mayker.

It overwelms me all o a sudden and I heeves into teers and I kno thats frownd upon see, got to be a man to work at Bearmouth. As I wype my fayce, I feels the scar on my nose, man enuff to work here I thinks, but I dunt cayre no more as the wet falls down my fayce and splish splashes onto the sheet coverin poor Tobe.

I turn and Thomas grabs me and holds me so tyte I fear I myte burst and I sob and sob and sob til all the waters gone fayre out o me and none o them say nothin but just let me cry and cry til Im all cryed out.

He stays here wi us this eve, says Skillen, voyce tremblin. We owe him that at leest.

Thomas looks to Jack who nods.

Ill report it in the mornin, says Skillen. Hes my lad, my trayler, tis for me to do.

Id never thawt o death lyke this. I seen axidents shore but when tis yore pal, yore bruvver almost, tis a very diffrent thing. And I feel so angry, my fists clentch not just at Walsh but at the Mayker too. How can he let somethin lyke this happen? How can this be any part o his plan? What kind o crewlty can be in the Maykers mind to let a thing lyke this happen to a boy so harmless and sweete and such a hard worker?

When I lies in bed that nyte, I think o what happend to Tobe. That mark round his neck, that bruse on his fayce. And I feels that self sayme anger wellin up inside me all over. Pure red hot anger.

And theres that little word again. Echoin round my head. Why? I keep askin myself. Why? Why dint the Mayker stop this? Why ent Walsh struck down for being an evil barstard? Why?

And I dare think it. I do. I dare think the unthinkaball, the unsayaball. What if.

What if the Mayker dunt cayre two hoots bout us see? And I think o the rock and the Maykers Hall and his fayce high up that you got to skwint at and I start askin all the questions then.

All those prayers and all those songs and all those amens. What if they is as much use as hot air see?

And I allow myself to think it.

What if the Mayker ent listernin? What if he ent even there? And my heart beats so fast and yet nothin happens, I ent struck down and the dorm dunt fall down on me and there ent a voyce from up high tellin me not to think such thawts or nothin lyke that.

And I think on and on and on til there ent no more thinkin to be dun and my mind is as clutterd and packd full o thawts as Bearmouth is packd full o coal.

But Ive thawt it now and if the Mayker dos see evrythin then he knos what Ive been thinkin. And for once in my life I ent scared o him neether. Cos if he left poor Tobe to be strangld and drownd and scared for his life and he dunt do nothin then tis only fayre that I ask myself these things.

Hello, I says in my head. Hello Mayker. I ent shore I believe in you no more, I says. Can you send me a sine? And I wayte and I wayte and nothin comes. Just thawts and thawts jumblin and swirlin lyke oyle in a puddle o water. Mixin and twirlin.

I feel the nyfe cold under my pillow and I holds it tyte.

MOUSE IS SAT ON TOBE WHEN I WAYKES UP AND LYTES A CANDUL. At leest tis what I thawt I saw. I rubs my eyes to wayke up and theres a movement, a flash o fur that disappeers out o the doorway.

He cayme back, I whispers to Tobe. He cayme back for you. And I do find some small comfort in that at leest.

When the uvvers arise, Skillen taykes Tobe up the levels to Mr Sharp. He goes on his own as we ent alloud to go up levels lyke that wi out permishun sayve on Maykers Day and you dunt get time off when someones died neether. Their body gets tayken away and any coinage left over sent to their famly if they has any. And thats it. Lyke Tobe ent ever eggsisted. Just gone. Vanished. Whooshed away.

I thawt I was used to death down here but I ent. Not now. Wi Tobe gone I wonders why any o us are here. I dunt go to letters wi Thomas but sits in a quiet dead end on my own in the dark and eats my stale crust on my own sharin bits wi any rats that dares come close tho I kno none o em are Mouse. I keeps turnin over thawts in my mind lyke a grayte weel. Whats the poynt o learnin letters when I ent ever goin to use em cept on letters to Ma?

I keep thinkin o Tobe, what happend to him. Those marks round his neck. That ent no axident, I think to myself. That ent no axident whatso evver. But why wuld anyone do that to Tobe? Hes just a young. He ent no trubble.

I hears a noyse comin down the rolley road near to

93

where Im sat and I jump all full o nerves and the lyke. I ent never been lyke this afore and now I find my hand tytely on the nyfe that Thomas gayve me last nyte.

The steps come closer and I see theres a lyte too and Im less scared then than I was. In the darkness anyone can be anythin. I herd tales o men forcin thereselves on youngs and on wimmin too fore they was banned from mines. I herd tales o wimmin givin birth while still on shift droppin it out from there bellyes onto the floor o the mine.

But the lyte gives me confeedents and I steps out into it only to almost walk into Devlin.

You alryte? he says. Been lookin for you, have me and Thomas.

I look at my feet.

Devlin reetches out a hand.

I dunt bite, he says. I kno what tis lyke to lose a loved one.

I looks up at him.

My Pa, he says. He was a good man he was.

Tobe was a good lad, I says as it hits me again. The thawt o never seein him again and I feels lyke doublin over in payne.

Yes. He was, says Devlin.

The whissul goes for end o brayke. Devlin holds his hand out still and I waytes for a moment. But the Mayker dunt show a sine I shouldunt tayke it so I wonder what myte happen if I do. His warm hand feels lyke a shock goin throo my evry nerve. And Mayker forgive me if yore even there still but I lyked it. I lyked evry moment our fingers was intertwynd I did.

I want to talk to Devlin more, about his Pa, about all o it but Im scared too. Im drawn to him lyke the white fish are drawn to folk swimmin in the layke but praps tis the Maykers way o testin me. Seein if Im loyal to him lyke Im sposed to be or else a heethen.

Arfter shift I catch site o Devlin as he washes under the pumps and I feels hot and odd and shayme.

At mess, the absence o Tobe on our bench is the blackest hole o all.

Walsh ent at mess nor at the pumps neether. Skillen says he reportd that Tobe was under Walshs command and we all o us hope and cross our fingers tyte as anythin that he ent comin back.

Maybe hes an awkwud man now, I says hopefully and Thomas nods.

Maybe, he says not soundin too shore.

The uvvers nod too but I can tell none o us do feel thatll be the cayse. Speshully at nyte when Thomas pulls the wooden panel across the dorm when we are almost all at bed.

Best be cayreful, he says.

Best be sayfe, says Jack.

Aye, the uvvers murmer. Aye. Best be sayfe.

Jacks coff coffin keeps us all up til he finally dozes off into snuffles. I lies awayke, think thinkin on evrythin. Tobe and Mouse and Rickerbee and him. Devlin. And the Mayker too. Til my thawts all merge into darkness and I finally drift off.

WHEN I WAYKES IN THE MIDST O THE NYTE, THERE IS DAMPNESS TWIXT MY THYES. I can feel it thick and odd not lyke piss.

I dunt kno what to do if trooth be told so I close my eyes tytely for a while and wish it away but when I opens them again tis still there. It smells straynge not lyke piss. Lyke mettal or somethin.

I sit up in bed and dunt kno whevver to larf or cry. I wayte and wayte but it ent goin away.

Thomas is the most learned man I kno so in the end I quietly gets up and I tippy tose over to him and gentlee tap him til he waykes.

Somethin has happend, I whispers.

What? he says alert as anythin.

Tween my legs, somethin straynge. Likwid.

Gather yore bedclothes, he whispers. Sheet and all. Quiet too, dunt wayke the uvvers.

I untuck my sheets and pull em out rollin em into a ball.

Quick, whispers Thomas as he quietly pulls open the wooden panel across the door cayrefullee layin it back arfter we steps out.

What we doin? I whisper.

Goin to the layke, he whispers back. Quick and quiet.

We both knos the way in the dark but Thomas taykes my hand and pulls me along wi him. I can feel theres a candul in his hand too, smooth against my parm.

I feel scared. I dunt kno what tis happenin but my heart tis fayre in my mouth.

When we get to the layke, Thomas stops and checks all round to mayke shore we are on our own.

He lytes the candul and holds it up to my groyne and I see there is brown red all round lyke I have hurt myself and I gasp.

Do not be conserned, says Thomas. It ent yore fawlt this has happend. Shh now and dunt panick, he says.

I put my hand tween my legs and see that the wetness I felt is thick and slippery. Blood. Thick blood comin from Mayker only knos where. Is this a punnishment for not bein loyal to the Mayker? Is this the sine I asked for?

I go to screem but Thomas clamps his hand over my mouth.

No Newt, he whispers hard at me. You screem and we are both dun for.

I ENT WHO I THAWT I WAS SEE.

All else is topsee and turvee.

I AM SUFFRIN FROM THE MONTHLEES THOMAS CALLS IT. Which
do meen that I ent who I thawt I was. It meens I ent a lad
arfter all but a gel. And we all kno that they hold no truck wi
gels down here.

I ent shore I is ever goin to get over the shock if trooth
be told but I ent ever growin the sossagemeet twixt my legs,
Thomas says. Insted I must bleed from my very inners once
a month.

And worst o all I must keep it seekret. From evryone,
from Jack and Will and Joe and Skillen. From Devlin. From
evryone.

I ent wantin this, I says to Thomas. I ent wantin this at
all but seems I ent got a choyce in the matter.

I AM FULL O FURY FOR THE MAYKER. Why dos he mayke gels bleed in this way?

It ent a punnishment, says Thomas, all gels and wimmin must have it at some stayge. Tis how it is. Dogs have it an all, he says. It ent just people. Tis the monthlees and tis natchural. Tis all my fawlt Newt, he says.

I ent ever seen Thomas cry afore but he dos this nyte.

I knew you wunt a lad in the first few days you was here, he says. But gels down here, they get passd round lyke a playthin mongst the worst kind o men. Tis how it was and tis how it is so I lied to you, lied to evryone sayin you ent one thing or tuvver. I been lyin to you for years, tis the only way I could keep you sayfe see. I been hopin and prayin that this day ent comin any time soon but here tis, he says. Do you forgive me?

I reetches out to him and holds him tyte as I can. It ent Thomass fawlt. He keeps me sayfe from harm. I cryes on his sholder for a bit but cryin dunt help matters.

More chaynges will come too, he says, and then I ent shore I can protekt you from it. Yore chest will swell and then there ent no hydin you cos yule be playne to see at the pumps in front o evryone at wash time arfter shifts. But we got a bit o time first see, we will think o somethin.

I dunt ryte kno what to think. I am releeved that the cramps ent me bein sick but I ent who I thawt I was. I ent what I thawt I was.

I am Newt still. I am me throo and throo. But I ent
no lad.

I feel rayge and fury for the Mayker but I dunt feel no
rayge for Thomas. I think back to those storyes I herd tell
o wimmin being forced on down here and I am in trooth
fayre grayteful that he lookd arfter me all this time.

But I must fayce things as they are now. I am a gel and
not yet a wimmin and yet this is a wimminlee thing that
I now suffers from.

I must use spayre cloth to wedge up tyte tween my legs to
soke up what blood there be and chaynge it when I can. But
I must be xtra cayreful at wash time so as no blood be seen
anywhere on me.

Thomas promisses to help find rags for me. But we start
wi my old sheet. Rip rip it up we do, tearin it apart and
tearin off the bloody bits til only the clene bits are left.

Thomas says I must burn the rags arfter so as none kno.
He says I carnt hide em cos o the rats so we lytes the blooded
rags from whats left o the sheet and watch it turn into teeny
flaymes bryte oringe and red and flick flickrin and I watch
all I thawt I was turn to ashes too.

MAYKERS DAY DOS FLY PAST LYKE A BLURRD DREAM HARF REMEMBERD HARF FORGOT. I am diffrent in ways I never knew before. I looks around the Hall at all the fayces sing singin and I wonders if they can see me. See who I really am. What I really am.

I looks up at the Mayker and skwints so as I can see his fayce properlee. All the questions tumball in my head lyke coal out a basket. Thomas keeps his hand on my sholder as we sings and I feel better for it, the cramps are less today.

The canduls flicker around the Hall wi the breath o hundreds o men and lads. All o us singin to him. And I the only gel.

Arfter prayers we go to the layke. I ent swimmin in it today, not wi the monthlees and not arfter what happnd to Tobe.

I sit at the edge and listern to the layke insted lap lap lappin. I dips my tose in and lets the blind fish nibble at em.

I cut my hair as short as I can wi the nyfe that Thomas gayve me. Thomas offers to do it for me but I must needs do it myself. Tis hard work and I cut my skalp a few times.

When I am dun, I look at my reflekshun in the layke and I look lyke I always did. A Bearmouth boy. Scar on my nostril, eyes starin back at me but my fayce feels lyke a mask wi the real me hidden behind. I kno that boy ent who I am no more. I am Newt and I am a Bearmouth gel.

DEAR MA

I am well and I hope you are too. I ent shore you are gettin these letters but tis good praktiss to write them anyways.

I kno it costs to write wi payper and ink and all and the ~~postidge~~ postage but Id lyke to kno how you are and how Auntie Soo is and evryone else.

Tobe ent wi us no more neether. He drownd but I ent shore that was all it was trooth be told as Walsh, one o the manidgers, it was on his watch and Tobe had marks round his neck and all. Mayke o that what you will eh.

Theres a new lad too in our dorm nayme o Devlin. I thawt he was odd at first but now I think hes alryte.

Ent much else to say this end sayve I love you and hope you love me too and think o me when my coinage gets sayfely to you.

I am growin up fast says Thomas who also sends his best regards.

Please write back. Please.

Love as always

Newt

NEWT COOMBES. Newt Coombes, says Mr Sharp in a loud voyce at gruel on Beer Munday.

I dunt put my hand up ryte away lyke cos I harf forget that a trayler dos tayke there haggers surnayme and I ent used to hearin folk say it out loud see.

Walsh stands up in the mess hall and poynts at me.

Over there Mr Sharp, he says. That one I do believe.

You ent taykin Newt, growls Jack under his breath and Mr Sharp smyles at him.

It ent for the Deep, he says. The Master wants to see this one is all.

The mess goes ryte quiet all around us.

The Master, the Master, the whispers start up.

The Master? I says and Mr Sharp nods.

Says so dint I? Ryte away too so hurry up cos he ent a man to keep waytin.

Thomas taykes my hand in his. Tayke cayre Newt, he says, skweezin my hand.

My heart is fayre in my mouth as I leeves the mess hall and follows Mr Sharp long the rolley roads and up the next level. I ent shore where we is goin xactly but Mr Sharp he walks fast and tis a job to keep up wi him.

The Master hisself, Mr Johnson, the mythikal creeture. But Thomas did meet him and he was real and so I must meets him too. But my heart is all a flutter thinkin o why the Master myte want me, what bisness he could possiblee hav wi the lykes o me.

Faster and faster Mr Sharp walks as we go up and up past whole swaythes o the mine that I ent ever seen before. Groups o uvver men and lads and ponys work workin away, doin the sayme jobs as me but levels up. Colder it gets as we go up and the men ent workin harf dressd lyke most are on my level but fully dressd wi clothes on their top harf too.

Tis lyke a miracle to me that we all fits into the Maykers Hall, all these men, all these lads and I wonders if there are uvvers lyke me here. Uvver gels pretendin to be lads too. I want to stop and ask about their pumps and dorms, their mess halls and evrythin but Mr Sharp he just keeps on walkin walkin and I have to fayre run to keep up wi him.

The hyte o the mines is taller here too and you dunt have to croutch in the sayme way but I kno this ent the way to the Maykers Hall. Tis lyke a verytabel mayze lyke Thomas told us once in one o his storyes about a harf man harf beest and a mayze and a ball o string and I harf wonders if tis me who should have thawt to bring somethin wi me to find my way back.

We keep goin up and up and up along grayte long steepe roads and I loses track o what level we can even be on when the lyte becomes so steddy and bryte that it hurts my eyes.

Lecktrik, I breethes and Mr Sharp nods.

Wayte here for a moment to allow yore eyes to ajust, he says.

And I blink blinks at lytes far bryter than in the Maykers Hall, lytes that dunt flicker neether.

Lyke magick ent it? I whispers and Mr Sharp snorts ryte throo his nostrils and a bit o snot comes out.

Dunt always work, he says wipin the snot away wi a hankercheef. Tis unrelyaball tis what it is.

I skwints and blinks at the lytes and they seems too bryte

for me to ever get customed to but Mr Sharp is off again and I follows him as best I can, blinkin as I do so.

Mr Sharps offiss is cold compayred to my floor. His is one o a series o wooden doors set deep into the rock. I counts em on my fingers—nyne in total. His door has a glass panel wi the word Overseer spelld onto it and Mr Sharp underneeth that. He sees me lookin at the letters and larfs.

Tis yore readin and writin and yore cleverness that dos bring you here, he says wi a grin fore he opens the door and ushers me throo.

The Master's back is to me as I step in and he warms hisself by a small fire in the corner as if it wunt hot enuff as tis but there he is. Mr Johnson, spinky blue suit and lyke Thomas says a tall hat as high again as his own head.

The whole room is coverd in wood see, panels and panels o it all carvd lyke a gentilmans house, lyke magick. Theres a grene bayze coverd desk near the fire wi chayres eether side o it. Tis a syte to see and I dunt rytely kno what to look at first til Mr Sharp cleers his throte and the Master turns around.

LEEVE US, HE SAYS COMMANDIN LYKE AND HE WAYVES HIS RIST WI A FLIKK AS IF MR SHARP WERE NO MORE THAN A TEENY BUZZIN FLY. Mr Sharp bends in two, doffin his own cap as he goes out backwuds, shuttin the door behind him.

The Master eyes me. He has a pinchd fayce wi poynted cheekbownes and a long nose. All beek and sharp and clever.

Sit, he commands and I do so on one o the chayres next to the big desk. He dunt sit hisself but watches me. He taykes his hat off and his hair underneeth is skwish skwashd flat black lyke a beetall wing.

Newt, he says slowlee, chewin over it. Funny nayme. Newt.

It ent my berth nayme Sir, I says. Niknayme from Thomas in my dorm but tis what Im known as now.

He smyles at me but his eyes narrow.

Confeedent little thing arnt you, he says.

I says nothin.

Yore letter, he says and he poyntes to the desk where a pile o letters sits. I can see my writin on the top sheet. My letter to Ma.

You mayke a seeriuss allegayshun in yore letter boy, he says finger tap tappin the letter.

I says nothin.

See Newt Coombes, you say in it that you suspect fowle play in Tobe Williamss death. Can you splayne yoreself to me please? he says matter o fact lyke.

There was marks round his neck Sir, I says. Cleer as day.

But it was reportd as an axident wasunt it?

Marks round his neck and drownd at the sayme time Sir, I says. A lad killin hisself two ways at the sayme time. Seems awfull funny dos that.

But I am not larfin, says the Master. Am I?

No, I mumbles.

Speke up boy, he says sharp lyke.

No Sir, I says cleerly.

He taykes a deep breath and then a big sigh. See I run a tyte ship here, he says, his finger tap taps on the letter. And I wuld very much lyke to improve the sayftee o this mine I wuld yet tis spensive so I have to ballents things up. Do I bring lectrick down to the furthest deeps knowin that twill be a wayste o money as the coal runs dry or should I rely on canduls down there?

He payces up and down.

Should I bring sayfety lamps down all parts o the mine when xpeerients says they arnt so sayfe arfter all? Should I equip all my workers wi better boots? He pauses for a moment. So many dialemmas you see that I fayce. So many. So should I promoat a man who seems very good at his job or should I get rid o him cos there are roomars about his behayvyer? What should I do Newt Coombes hmm? he says.

You talkin bout Walsh Sir, I says. That it?

He smyles at me. Walsh gets things dun Newt, one o the most produktiv manidgers Ive had here in a long time. So tell me, do I throw that away cos o one or two, shall we say, misdemeenurs or do I let it slip and leeve things as they are?

I says nothin.

The reputayshun o Bearmouth rests upon all o us here,

he says. Mayker protekt us. And many o the things Id lyke to do here I carnt cos o the cost. And Bearmouth has got to be competittiv in todays markit. You understand?

I says nothin.

See Newt, it has come to my attenshun that you and the men in yore dorm, they have the potenshul to mayke trubble in the mine. You understand yes?

I says nothin.

One o them, Thomas is it, who I believe is the one who teeches you yore letters, and very nycely too I may say, he askd for a payrise. You understand that at leest?

I nod. But I still says nothin.

And Devlin, he says. What o that young man eh?

And Mayker forgive me if yore even there but I blush to my tippy tose.

Ah, says the Master watchin me wi his hawk eyes. Ah. Stand up, boy, he says wi his head on one side and I do so.

He comes over to me ryte up close and peers at me, fayce and beeky nose just inches away from me.

What a pretty thing you are, he says whisperin slowlee. And you lyke boys too yes? His hand reetches out and smooths my cheek. Not even a thin layer o down on it yet, he says. You are so young yoreself. A mere chylde is all.

His hand goes down my fayce and down my nek and tis cold his hand and I shivers. It stops on my chest in the mid and he holds his hand out flat against me. I fear for my life if he finds the nyfe that Thomas gayve me tyte in my pockit and I pray to the Mayker to sayve me even tho I ent trooly shore hes there no more.

But he stops there dos the Master. Hand on my chest lookin at me. Waytin.

The fire crackels in the grayte and he taykes his hand

away and strokes my cheek again. He keeps his eyes on me still.

Such a pretty little thing, he mutters as he turns back to the desk and sits down. Sit, he commands again, wayvin his hand and so I do, heart thud thuddin in my chest and I realizes I been holdin my breath all the time.

See Newt, he says. You could be very useful to me. Devlin is I think a bad inflooents and I think it wuld be advisaball for me to keep an eye on him. You understand?

I says nothin.

I only alloud him to come here cos o his farver, says the Master and then larfs to hisself. Im sorry, he says, the smyle wyped clene off his fayce. Just a little joke for my own amewsment. He reetches into his pockit and taykes out a coin, a real one, a shiny spinky clene goldern one so bryte it maykes me blink and he playces it cayrefullee on the desk in front o me.

See Newt, I could pay for informayshun about such things, he says quietly. I could pay handsumlee.

He slides the coin over towards me and trooth be told I ent ever seen such ritches in all my life. I swallows.

I am a direkt lyne to the Mayker, he says. A deesendant from the Mayker hisself so tis only ryte that you do what I ask. He smyles at me.

I hear his clok tick tickin to itself and the fire crackels and spits.

I got to be cayreful here, real cayreful see, I thinks to myself. I taykes a deep breath.

But there ent nothin to spy on tho Sir, I says and I tremballs as I do so. Thing is Sir, Thomas askd for a payrise and one was not forthcomin so tis the end o that.

And Devlin he is merelee settlin in still. He ent tayken to bein a Bearmouth boy easy lyke but he will in time Im shore.

The Master looks at me as if hes tryin to see ryte throo me. He tuts to himself.

You understand Newt, no informayshun, no coin. He puts his finger out and slip slides the coin back towards hisself.

All o them ritches tayken away from me.

I wish there was somethin I could say Sir, I says. But I ent a liar and I ent goin to tayke money for lyin neether.

Ah, an honest pup, he says. Tis a cryin shayme tho as it dos meen I have to do this to yore letter home. I do hope you understand.

He taykes my letter and drops it lyke a fether into the fire and whoomph tis gone. A flicker o lyte and my writin dos turn to ashes.

I starts up but he motions me back to the chayre.

You see Newt, I must protekt the reputayshun o Bearmouth, he says smylin at me. So yore Ma must wayte for anuvver letter mustent she?

He leans across the desk. If you have anythin else to tell me chylde I suggest you say it now.

He leans back, arms folded tyte across his chest and waytes.

I says nothin as the twigs and sticks do spit and crackel in the fire.

Shayme, he says. Then he breethes in quick lyke and stands up wi a sigh.

You had yore chance, he says. I gavye you chances today, opportewnitees Coombes and it was _you_ who didunt tayke em. Remember that.

He watches me for a moment. And I dunt kno ryte what to say to that so I says nothin, rayge growin in me at the thawt o my letter turnd to flaymes.

Sharp, he bellows and Mr Sharp comes runnin in.

We are dun here, he says. Return the chylde to where you found him.

Mr Sharp grabs my arm and fayre drags me out o there fore I can say anythin else. I want to spit in the Masters fayce I do, burnin my letter lyke that, tryin to get me to spy on my frends.

But his words echo round my head and my mouth is all dry.

But I kno what else I sees in there too. All them uvver letters, a whole pile o em stackd high on the desk. And I bets to myself that they are from uvver workers down here see. I bet they are. And he or Mr Sharp or someone has opend all o em to see whats bein sed about em. Usin em for spyin, usin em for their own purposses.

I feel angry but calm somehow. And I sees it cleerly now. The answers to the whys I been askin. The Maykers way is for the Masters gayne. The Mayker ent for us, the Mayker is for the Master. The Mayker, he ent even listernin. Not to me, not to any o us. Not for years and maybe, just maybe, he ent ever been listernin.

My mind feels lyke a teeny tiny chick braykin out o its shell.

There is a fire in my belly and lyke the pheenix in Thomass storyes, I am reborn anew.

AS MR SHARP RETURNS ME TO THE LOWER LEVELS MY BRAYNE TRYES TO TAYKE IN ALL THAT I SEE. There are more men down here than I ever seen in one go on the uvver side, fore I cayme to Bearmouth. I think o all the men in the Maykers Hall, hundreds o em, singin and prayin in the grayte Hall.

We ent alloud to mix wi uvver levels sayve on Maykers Day see, and we ent alloud more than can fit seated in caban to gather in any one go neether. Tis the rules o Bearmouth. But still Im thinkin it. There are so many men and yet so few manidgers. I counted no more than nyne doors incloodin Mr Sharps offiss. Addin it up, workers outnumbers overseers and manidgers by an awfull lot. An awfull lot.

And I think o what Devlin sed all that time ago. It taykes one person. Just one.

So many men and boys down here workin away flesh to bone and me the only gel. I puts my hand over my pockit and feels the chill smoothness o the nyfe that Thomas gayve me.

I will remember evrythin I see on my way back down. Evrythin.

Cos one person can be got rid o see and I fear tis what the Master is arfter, I fear he will hand me to Walsh for the Deep. I fear he is the one who will come for me. But I needs must tell the uvvers what I have seen, what I have herd. You may get rid o me but you carnt get rid o evry man, you carnt get rid o men thinkin diffrent to how youd lyke em to. Can you?

MR SHARP TAYKES ME BACK TO MESS BUT ALL THE MEN ARE GONE.

You kno yore way from here, he says and leeves me, belly rumblin at thawt o gruel but knowin that tis all gone for the day. Ent even pickd a crust for layter neether. But I got uvver things to think about now.

I nods to him, hand in my pockit and I heads down into the tunnels in the darkness lyke a mole to find Jack.

I needs must be cayreful now see, I do think to myself on my way down, listernin for footsteps and the lyke. Tis not only those in my dorm who has mayde enemees wi Walsh, seems to me we has also now mayde enemees wi the very Master hisself.

I think o the letter to Ma burn burnin up in the grayte and my fists clentch.

Coinage on payper, coinage on ink, coinage on postidge. Up in smoke. And worst o all Ma wunt hear nothin from me for anuvver six months now. I growl to myself and hear it round me.

If yore angry, Thomas told me once, if yore angry, tis best that you bottal it up, keep it focussd lyke and then use it for somethin.

Tis what Ill do wi this new found rayge. I will use it so help me. Ill use evry last drop o it.

JACK IS SHORE PLEASED TO SEE ME WHEN I TURN UP. Hes strugglin on his own to both fill the basket and chip chip away at the coal but the two o us gets the work dun in harf the time.

Whyd the Master want to see you then? says Jack.

He wantd me to spyes on you all, I says. For coinage.

Spyes on us? says Jack stoppin what hes doin. Spyes on us for what? Whats anyone got to say bout us?

Theres plenty o time for talkin layter, I says. Arfter mess when we is all back in dorm. Things for all o us to consider.

I can feel Jack lookin at me diffrentlee.

You alryte Newt? he says and I nod.

I am, I says. And I ent no spy neether. We ent always been best o frends Jack, trooth be told, but we is loyal to each uvver and tis what matters in the long run. But I been thinkin a lot see and I thinks we need to get plannin is all. See tis playne to me now, the Master lykes Walsh, he as much as sed so cleer as day, and Walsh dunt lyke us a jot and so—

I leeves it hangin in the air see.

Alryte, says Jack. Alryte. Dorm talk wi all o us Newt. Alryte.

And tis back to work lyke nothin ever happend. Slog sloggin away and all to put coins in the pockit o him up there. The Master wi his spinky clothes and his tall hat.

Direkt lyne to the Mayker is what he sed. But I dunt think he even believes in him.

I works hard that mornin, we counts up we dun nyne fore the whissul goes and I heads to letters.

Thomas hugs me soon as he sees me. He holds me tyte to him. Devlins there too lurkin in the dark. He gives out a sigh o relief when he sees me and runs his hands throo his hair lyke.

What happend? says Thomas and I tells em all. Evry last drop o it. Evry word the Master says, the letter burnin, the uvver parts o Bearmouth I ent ever seen fore, lecktrik lytes, all o it tho Thomas dos kno some parts from his own trip to the Master see.

Devlin shaykes his head when I tells o what the Master says about his Pa. About that bein why Devlins here. He bangs his fist against the wall. Thomas puts a hand on him.

Calm calm, he says. Calm yoreself so we can think rashunally about all o this.

Calm, says Devlin angry lyke. Calm. That man . . . I swear.

Yore farver is dead tho ent he? I says.

Hes dead cos o Mr Johnson, Devlin says.

Tell Newt the trooth, says Thomas.

Alryte, Devlin says. He thinks for a while fore he starts.

My Pa was settin up a group o men topside to protesst for better workin condishuns for men down Bearmouth and the uvver mines. Sayin tis no better than slayveree down here for men and boys. Bein vokal about it he was, goin to villidge halls and the lyke. Started gettin a head o steme up on it all.

Then one day these men turns up dressd in suits and they taykes him away sayin they was wi the awthoritees and wantd to question him. My Ma goes wild when she finds out, goes arfter em but hes disappeerd into thin air. Ent no awthoritee clayms to have him.

But he myte still be—I says but Devlin interrupts me, shaykin his head.

No, he says. Fishurman found his body down the bottom o the gorge not two weeks layter. Brused and blooded.

And, says Thomas. Promptin him to say more.

And wi marks round his neck, Devlin says, tho the thawt o this dos cleerly woond him as he says it. Marks lyke a liggatchur, he says.

And I thinks back to Tobe. I thinks back to holdin him in my arms that eve by the layke. Those marks around his neck.

Tis what they do to those who dare disagree, Devlin says. Tis how it is. They have all the power in their hands and they will do anythin to keep it that way.

But Tobe wunt doin no body no harm, I says.

But Walsh is frends wi the Master, says Devlin. That much seems cleer from what you say. And the fact Mr Johnson did joke about it too, about my Pa, says a lot for the manner o the man.

What did he meen about you bein here as a fayvour then? I says.

Go on, says Thomas.

Devlin taykes deep breaths forcin hisself to tell me.

It ent a pretty story, he says, not lyke the ones Thomas tells you.

Im old enuff to hear the trooth, I says and Thomas nods.

Arfter what happend wi Pa, we struggled, me and Ma and my younger bruvvers, Devlin says. We startd to go hungree. Ma couldunt find any work, where so ever she asked, she got turnd down again and again. Cleenin, millin, helpin out on odd jobs, nothin. It was lyke the walls o the whole villidge cayme down. So she tryes the next villidge and the next and it was the sayme. Time and time again.

Why? I says.

Cos the villidgers rely on the mines, for work for coinage. They carnt afford to stir up trubble so they keeps quiet.

What happend then? I says. Lyke how you ends up here.

Mr Johnson cayme to Ma wi an offer. Not him o corse, Devlin says. Not the man hisself, one o his lackees. Send me down the mine and Id earn enuff for em to get by. My bruvvers were starvin. Ma didunt want me to come but I left for here the next day. Took me three whole days o walkin to get here but then when I arrived they beat me. Whippd my back til it fayre drippd blood.

I remember, I says, when you first cayme to the layke, I remembers the weals on yore back.

Devlin looks down at the floor. I thawt if I could just get down here, see what it was lyke for myself, I could perswayde uvver men to see what Pa could see. Carry on his good work. Try and do somethin. But the darkness, the lack o air. I thawt I was goin mad at first. Those first days were the hardest I have ever known. But then I rememberd Pa, thawt what he wuld o dun. He wuld not give up so eesily. So I hardend my resolve. I could not fail him. I wuld not fail him. I wuld get out, tell the world what I had seen. What it was trooly lyke down here.

It taykes one person, tis what you sed to me back then. Tis why you tryd to escaype, I says and he nods.

There are guards on evry level, he says. Eyes and ears evrywhere. I am not so used to the dark as you, I carnt use it to my advarntidge. I wasunt hard to catch. And when they did, they beat me. Kept me in a small dark room for I dunt rytely kno how long. Fed me stale bred and beat me. Devlin goes quiet. I failed him, he says. I failed my Pa.

No, I says. No. Cos yore still here. And we can still do somethin. This ent the end Devlin, I says. Tis only the beginnin, ent that ryte Thomas?

Thomas looks thawtful.

I fear for us, he says. I fear for all o us but this lad here has askd me questions that have fayre chaynged the way I see things. And it wuld be a poor man who didunt want to act on it. Tis why I went to see the Master.

But yet nothin has chaynged, I say. Not yet anyways. I taykes a deep breath. Tis time I told you both somethin, I says.

And I tells em both about Rickerbee, about what me and Tobe saw, and Thomas nods, his fayce seeriuss.

I herd a man had been banishd from anuvver part o the mine, says Thomas. An awkwud man, moved on some time ago. Perhaps twas the sayme man you saw Newt.

Devlin nods. Beaten up lyke they beat me fore they let him go eh, he says.

I hold out my hand and Devlin puts his on myne, lookin strayte into my eyes and Thomas puts his hand on top. Three hands. Together.

And I thinks to myself too, at the back o my head, I ent ever herd Devlin talk so much before.

AT THE PUMPS ARFTER WORK, I KEEPS MY HEAD DOWN BUT WALSH IS THERE AND I SEES HIM LOOKIN AT ME, EYES BORIN THROO ME. I ignores him as best I can. Our dorm group sticks tyte together now and we walks as one to mess. Arfter our meet and tatties, the grayte beer barrels are brawt in, rolly rolly for Beer Munday.

Tis time we went but as Thomas, me and Devlin go to stand, Walsh is there, swift as an eel and ryte by us.

Where are you goin then? he says. These two are shore old enuff for beer ent they?

We do not answer to you, says Thomas. Kindly move out o our way.

Walsh holds eye contact for a moment before steppin aside.

Watch yoreself learned man, he says. Watch yoreself. And them two. The Master has his eye on you, he says, lookin at me. He has his eye on you.

I feels sick arfter we leeve. The thawt o bein watchd, all the men drinkin thereselves to harf wits. I dunt feel lyke letters or talkin so I heads strayte back to dorm but Thomas and Devlin dunt feel tis sayfe leevin me on my own so they dos come back too and sits and talks in the corner. I hides myself under my blankit, wishin the world away. Wishin Bearmouth away. Wishin myself sayfe and tyte some uvver playce entirelee.

TIS THE NEXT DAY THAT TRUBBLE DOS COME TO PASS. Arfter
letters at brayke, I heads back to Jack and Devlin heads to
Skillen in the next sharft havin taykin over Tobes role.
Devlin walks me to the top o the rolley road where our paths
split and skweezes my hand to say fayrewell. My hand fayre
tingalls for some time arfter but then it comes.

Trubble.

Tis on the second basket up that it happens.

When I get to the top I hears it again. The footsteps
I herd before that time. Shufflin into the distance.
Someone who ent sayin nothin. My hand tytens on the nyfe
in my pockit. Still there.

Hello, I says, whisperin. But there ent no answer so
I dunt say it again. Praps tis my maginayshun is all.

I clamps the basket on, reddy to unload it, but he must o
snuck up craftee lyke under the noyse o the clamps cos all o
a sudden theres a hand over my mouth and a whiff o smelly
stinky beer breath.

Hello little mouse. Tis Walshs voyce, whisperin in my
ear. Little mouse sneekin around and up to no good dunt
deserve no chees, he whispers.

I bytes down on his fingers but hes fast and grabs me wi
his uvver hand, throwin his fingers in my mouth and down
my throte.

I gag and gag but hes twyce my size and got me held tyte
as anythin.

Little mouse is trappd, he says and I feel his tung in my ear lick lick lickin. Little mouse taystes so good, he says. Just lyke mouses frend did. O he told me all about his little pet in the end but I thawt twas an awfull good nayme for you an all eh mouse.

I kicks at him usin all my wayte to try and knok him off his feet so I can reetch for my nyfe but he is strong, stronger than me. I want to screem and cry but tis all I can do to breeth wi his fingers rammd down my throte and my arms held tyte behind me.

Dunt wriggall so mouse, he says as he licks my neck. Dunt wriggall so, he says sharply. He pulls me up and I feel cold thinness at my neck. A nyfe Im shore o it.

I go still and quiet.

See mouse, he whispers and the cold thinness goes away. That wunt so hard was it? He taykes his fingers out o my mouth and fore I can screem, he pushs me hard up gainst the rock fayce holdin my arms tyte behind me wi one hand, fayce pushed up gainst the ruff rock and Im gaspin for air.

I feel his uvver hand over me, over my buttocks and edge edgin at my trowsers tryin to pull em off. I tryes to screem but no noyse comes out.

Come on mouse, a mans got to have a bit o fun eh. And such a pretty young thing you are eh, tis what the Master says too. Think he was harf temptd to tayke you for hisself but he dun give you to me insted and for that I do thank him a thousund times.

All the time he is reetchin and pullin and I can feel a hard thing behind me lyke a large candul press pressin into my back.

His hand is slippd down twixt the cloth and my skin and I feel his hand stroke strokin me on the rear.

I wunt byte mouse, he murmers, well I myte eh.

I wriggalls and skwirms and dos my best to get free o
him, but he pushs gainst me hard and there ent no room.

How you do wriggall mouse, he says sharp lyke. More
than yore little frend did. He just stood stock still and let me
do whatever I so pleased to him so he did.

He pulls my trowsers down, rippin the cloth as he dos
so and I feels the breeze on my skin and his warm hand hot
and hevvy on me.

Yes mouse, he says groanin to hisself.

I feels his fingers slip slide betwixt my cheeks and I kno
then for certain that he dos plan to forss hisself on me.

In desperayshun, I gets my left arm free but he pushs
gainst me so hard it taykes all my strength to try and skweeze
my arm throo to reetch at the nyfe in my ryte pockit.

He reetches down twixt my thyes too.

What are you little mouse? he whispers, they calls you a
younuck dunt they eh? Twill be so sweete to tayste and plukk
one o them as I ent ever had a younuck afore.

I can feel him twixt my legs and I feel him pause a
moment as he finds the edge o the blooded clout bound tyte
for the monthlees.

Whats this eh? he says puzzld lyke, and he taykes his
wayte off me for just a moment.

Tis all I need. I wriggalls my ryte arm free and pulls the
nyfe from my pockit and I jabs backwuds gettin him strayte
in the leg as hard and deep as I can and jerks it strayte back
out again.

He stumbles back yellin wi payne and I taykes my chance.
I turns round, trowsers harfway fallin off and I goes at him
again wi the nyfe in the dark. I feels it sink into somethin
and a yell o payne and I knos I got him.

I pulls the nyfe back out, steps back in the dark and hides round the uvver side o the basket.

Think Newt think, I says to myself, heart hammerin in my ears. He wunt stop now. He wunt stop til you is dead and gone.

I breethes to myself as quiet as I can but my heartbeat dos sound lyke thunder and I wonder that the whole o Bearmouth carnt hear it echoin down the tunnels.

Where are you mouse? he says angry now but tryin to hide it. Voyce louder than before, no whispers now. Come here little mouse, tis only a joke eh. Ent goin to hurt you proper lyke was I now eh?

I kno this part o the road lyke the backs o my hands and I hears him lookin for me, waytin for me to give myself away but I ent goin to. Tis a fyte to the last and I must needs use my braynes to beat him for I shore ent got the strength to beat him in a strayte fyte.

I hears his footsteps come ryte close to me, the uvver side o the basket and I waytes, countin em as they comes nearer and nearer. Tis the only chance I has to get him.

Tis not til I feels the air from his walkin almost touch my fayce that I stabs him strayte in the leg again and again, jab jab, and I hears him toppall over backwuds.

Mouse has got a bad bite, he shouts. Wayte til the Master hears about this, you little barstard.

I hears him tryin to get back up but he has fallern bad lyke and I taykes my chance again.

Hes fallen over ryte by the far edge o the basket, I herd him fall. I gets up fast as I can and unclamps the basket as fast as I can clamp clamp clamp. Must be a hundred wayte o coal in it and I heeves and heeves and pushs it up and over and onto him. The whole load. Clutter clutter thud thud

thud it falls and falls on him pushin him down and down and drownin his voyce out. Suffokaytin him.

Silence.

I listerns and listerns but there ent nothin cept my own breethin in the darkness. Breethin in and out, in and out lyke a simpallton. In and out.

In.

Out.

Tis all I can manidge for now.

I pulls my rippd trowsers back up as best I can and shoves the blooded clout into my pockit along wi the nyfe.

I ent never killd a man before. I ent ever killd nothin before and now here tis.

I ent sorry bout it neether. He murderd Tobe he did and hed o dun me in and all if I hadunt stoppd him.

I goes to stand but my legs ent havin it and I wobballs back down to sittin. I feels wetness on my fayce and I ent shore if tis blood or tears when I wypes it wi my sleeve.

I dunt rytely kno what to do so I sits there for I dunt kno how long til a candul lyte comes dancin down the tunnel and I thinks to myself that all is lost and that I am fayre undun.

MAYKER SAYVE ME.

Tis Devlin unloadin his basket on the rolley road.

I hisses to him, more grayteful than any time since that he is still too feard o the dark to work wi out a candul.

He comes over strayte aways tho he carnt yet clap eyes on me.

Hello, he says. Anyone there? he says. Newt?

My legs still ent workin proper lyke but I cryes out and he holds the lyte up and sees me.

What happend? he says fayce full o horror. Yore fayce tis bleedin.

Walsh, I crokes out. Walsh.

Where is he? says Devlin. Where is he? His fayce tis full o rayge.

I poyntes to the pile o coal skwish skwashin him underneeth.

Is he . . . ?

I nods.

I taykes the nyfe out o my pockit and tis cleer that it dos have blood on it. I shows Devlin and he nods.

He tryes to. . . . He tryes to. . . . I starts to speke and I swallows but I carnt push the words out o my mouth, they stays cawt in the back o my throte.

But Devlin sees. His eyes go over the rippd trowsers and I see in his eyes that he understands.

He did it to Tobe, I whispers.

Devlin taykes a deep breath.

126

We needs must move him, he says. Fore anyone else sees him. Can you stand? he says and he offers me a hand.

I struggles but I gets up, legs wobblin lyke a newborn fole.

We must be quick, if someone else sees . . .

He leeves it hangin but I kno that we must hide what I have dun as fast as we can.

Thomas, I says. Thomas.

Devlin dunt understand at first.

The dynamyte, I says. Thomas, hes openin a new sharft and—

Devlin is alreddy movin the coal to one side, quick quick.

When do the next lot come to tayke this away? he says poyntin at the coal.

I ent shore, I says. I just brings it here and I dunt kno.

Think, he says. Twyce a day, three, fore what?

I dunt rytely kno, I says. I think tis collectd three times. Twas cleerd this mornin by letters so.

We must hurry, he says.

I helps as best I can but I am not ryte still so Devlin must work twyce as hard to cleer it. And then there he is. That fayce starin back at me. Walsh. Trickall o blood runnin down from his pale white forehead.

That fayce. Im tremblin all over and I carnt stop myself. I backs up against the rocks feelin em cold and wet behind me.

Devlin holds the candul over Walshs fayce lookin at those starin eyes til all o a sudden they looks towards him.

Devlin stumbles backwuds fayre near blowin out the lyte.

He ent dead arfter all.

Walshs mouth opens and closes lyke a fish but there ent no sound comin out o it.

What are we to do? Devlin whispers and we look at each uvver, panickd. Time dos stop still for a moment but then a rattlin sound dos come from Walshs mouth and his piggy meen eyes do roll backwuds ryte into his fayce. All is still. He is gone.

I kno who he is now, the shadow man. His voyce whisperin in my ear. That voyce shoutin at me. Twas the sayme voyce I herd all that time ago. Tis the man who orderd the beatin o Rickerbee. Tis the man who killd Tobe and who knos how many uvvers.

This little mouse bytes back, I thinks to myself but then I snorts and heeves and sniffals and sobs til Devlin dos shayke me.

We got to get out o here Newt, he says. Come on.

He pushs me gentlee to one side as I leans against the walls for support and he moves the coal fast and quick and silent to the side o the rails where it should be for the next lot to shift. There is blood all down both o Walshs legs, so much blood, and I knos I got him good and proper.

Help me, says Devlin. I carnt do it on my own.

And together we heeve Walsh into my basket and I carnt bring myself to look at his fayce.

Tis dun, I thinks to myself and I allows myself one deep breath. Tis dun and trooth be told I ent the leest bit sorry.

CAN YOU HEAR ME MAYKER?

I feel Walshs blood on my hand stick sticky and I feel queesee inside.

Tis I, and I have killd a man, I says in my head as Devlin and I push the basket down the rolley roads to where we hope beyond hope that Thomas will be.

Can you hear me Mayker? But there ent no reply.

We covers Walshs body in the basket wi coal so none will see him. Devlin pulls the basket at the front wi the candul wedgd in and I pushs at the back, hidden in the dark. There is blood on me. Over me. Sticky and crustd.

We pass uvver men in the mine, fayces I only see at mess and Devlin spekes for us both.

Mayke way, he says. Tis the Masters orders, he says. He calld to see this one at gruel yesterday as you may o herd and today this lad is on speshul orders.

Tis lyke a magick pass sayin such things and so we are let past wi out hindrants.

Devlin wyped my fayce clene as best he could but I can feel wi the stingin and the soreness that there must needs be a bloody big bruse comin.

It taykes what feels lyke forever fore we come to the area where Thomas is workin and Devlin must ask the way several times before we find him.

Tis lyke a mayze down here, says Devlin and he ent wrong.

Thomas is workin on his own openin up a new seam

and if it wernt for Devlins candul, Im shore wed have fayre scared him out o his wits turnin up lyke this.

Devlin dos all the talkin whilst I stand by the basket clutchin it tyte to hold myself upryte and thinkin about what I dun.

Mayker can you hear me?

Are you there?

But answer comes there none.

And then all I remember is darkness.

WHEN I WAYKES UP I AM IN MY OWN BED BUT I AM GRUBBEE AND NOT PROPER CLENE LYKE.

Then I remembers. What happend. What I did to Walsh.

It plays in my head again and again. Those hands over me, that fear risin in me. The panick as I tryes to wriggall free. Walsh. The man in the shadows. What I now kno he did to Tobe too.

They must o brawt me back. I must o clene faynted aways.

I feel sick and I goes to get up but I carnt.

I feels a hand on me.

No Newt. Lie back down. You ent reddy to get up.

Tis Devlin.

Where is evryone, what time is it? I says.

Tis still workin time, he says. We told Jack what happend and hes coverin for you. Skillens coverin for me too. Thomas told me to bring you back so I did.

Did it really happen? I whispers.

Yes, says Devlin.

I feel his hand wrap around myne. Warm.

Yore the brayvest person I ever did meet, he says. I dunt kno if Id the couridge to act lyke that so fast and all, he says. Yore a strong person Newt. Trooly you are.

I tryes to sit up a bit and Devlin perches on the side o my bed.

You alryte if I sits here? he says and I nod.

131

I swallows. I dunt want to think about it no more. None o it.

Tis all gone now, he says. Thomas has hidden him down the end o that tunnel hes blastin and twill all be gone by evenin. Blown to dust.

I nod.

Im sorry any o this happend, he says. Leest o all to you.

We sits there in silence for a moment.

Youd best get some rest, he says. And then he gets up and lets go o my hand.

Darkness closes in around me and I feel my hand reetch for my nyfe, fingers closin round it.

Tis alryte Newt, he says. Ill stay here til the uvvers come back.

I hear him go down to his bed and sit down. If you are in need o anythin, he says.

Thanks, I mumbles. Thanks for—

Dunt mentshun it, he says. Youd o dun the sayme for me. Twas just luck I filld my basket at the ryte time eh?

I lies there for ayges and in the distance I feel a faynt tremor o an xplosion judder throo me. And I taykes comfort in thinkin that tis the end o him, the end o the shadow man whevver tis Thomass dynamyte or some uvver bodys, it dos fayre give me comfort.

Bully Walsh wi his piggy eyes and his wandrin hands and his forcin hisself on who knos how many. But he is gone now. Dust lyke the coal itself.

And Mayker forgive me, murderer that I am, but I am awfull glad.

WHEN I NEXT WAYKES, THEY IS ALL COMIN BACK IN ARFTER MESS. Thomas has brawt me some meet and tatties in a cloth and altho I dunt think I have any appertyte I dos scoff the lot in one go.

A candul flick flickers in the dorm and the men, they all do look at me.

Mayker sayve you Newt, says Jack tryin to sound joviall lyke. Dunt think you was the one wuld rid us o that barstard but you dun a good job there I reckons. Best rid o him eh?

The Davidson twins nod silently.

Skillens fayce is calm but I can see he is full o fury.

To think what he did, he says suddenlee, forcin the words throo his teeth. To think he tryes to force hisself on you and Mayker only knos what he did to poor Tobe.

Thomas cleers his throte and all do look at him, me and Devlin, Skillen and Nicholson and the Davidson twins mewt as ever. Tis cleer that all the dorm do now kno both what I did and what Walsh did too.

There ent no body, not now at leest, and no way o pinnin it on us but I fear we will all be laybelld awkwud men from this poynte on, he says.

But it ent yore fawlt, I says. Ent the fawlt o none o us.

Tis what it is, says Thomas.

Aye, Jack nods.

My head fayre ayks wi it all and I touches my fayce and can feel the bruse risin up underneeth.

Newt is not well enuff to be diskussin such things, says Devlin watchin me, and Thomas sits next to me.

Lie down, he says, forget we are here. Rest up and we will tell you all in the mornin. Alryte? he says and I nods.

Thank you, I says to Devlin and he smyles at me.

And I wonders to myself as I turns over away from the lyte, hearin the mutter o the men behind me, my men, my dorm, my Bearmouth famly, why I did ever think he myte be the Devil?

THEY TALK, THE MEN, THEY TALK THROO THE NYTE BUT I AM TOO WORN THROO TO LISTERN IN PROPERLEE LYKE SO I FALLS ASLEEP AND DO SLEEP LYKE A BABE.

I must o slept for a fayre long time as I dunt waykes up til all are reddyin thereselves for gruel the next mornin.

You go, says Thomas to them all. We will catch you up.

He is cayreful to close the panel arfter em too fore he helps me chaynge into my clene clothes. I am stiff all over and stickee below from the monthlees but the blood is less than twas and tis not a bad job. Thomas dos think this will be the last day o it and for that I am glad.

Thomas dos tell me too that all in the dorm are sworne to seekrissee over what happend wi Walsh and I cross my fingers and hope he is ryte. They are my famly in a way tis troo but famly oft times dunt agree on all things. But he says they is all agreed and I must not worrye about it so I must needs leeve it.

Alryte? says Thomas when I am dressd and clene and I nod. He hugs me to hisself. You are a bravye chylde, he says. I am proud o you, Newt, he says. There is a spark in you that no one else got, you understand?

And I dunt really understand, not properlee but I nods anyways.

Good, he says, pattin me on my cheek gentil lyke.

Howd you kno so much about the monthlees? I says.

Thomas dunt look at me for a moment.

Had an older sister, he says.

I dunt kno that, I says.

We were close me and her, he says. He pauses for a moment think thinkin to hisself. Twas a long time ago. Anuvver life, he says.

We sits in silence for a moment.

Ryte, he says. Reddy Newt? he says and I nods and we head to mess.

WHEN WE TURNS UP MR SHARP IS ALREDDY DEEP IN CHAT WI WALSHS MEN FORE HE SEES US COME IN. He heads strayte for us.

Walsh, he says, any o you seen him?

I shaykes my head. Not since yesterdays gruel I think, I says. And my voyce dos hide my lyin awfull well.

I ent seen him since yesterday neether, says Thomas. Come to think o it, he wurnt at the layke arfter shifts. Has he chaynged shift praps?

Mr Sharp looks cross. No he ent, he says. He has playne disappeerd so he has and ent no one knos where to.

Mr Sharp looks at my fayce, at the brusin lyke.

Axident, I says. Should o been more cayreful on the rolley road, I says and Mr Sharp tuts and nods.

He turns to Jack and the rest. You seen Walsh since yesterday?

And they shaykes their heads and says no they ent.

It dos stryke me that we are all playne good liars and I ent shore if Im a little bit proud o that in all trooth.

Mr Sharp goes round all the uvver mess taybles askin if anyone has seen Walsh but none has.

One o his men comes up to us, I dunt kno his nayme.

Shore you ent seen him? he says to us.

Corse, says Jack wi a growl. We ent liars are we? Last I saw o him was here in mess. Eatin wi all you lot. So Im guessin yore the last folk he saw. Stands to reesun we should be askin you eh?

137

Skillen smyles and nods. Shore <u>you</u> ent seen him? Skillen says to Walshs man and the fella backs off and goes back to his tayble.

Thomas pats me on the back. Eat yore gruel Newt, he says. Will do you good.

Devlin eats harf o his and then passes it to me.

Shore? I says and he nods. So I eat his and all and fayre lick it out o the bowl.

I look around at the fayces from the dorm—learned Thomas, daft barstard Jack, tuff hard Skillen, the twins Will and Joe, fayces fayre identikal and both quiet as mice, Nicholson all sinnew and mussall and then Devlin wi his handsumness and kindness and then, heart sinkin to tippy tose, the playce where Tobe sat.

They are all my famly these fellas. They are my world.

When we heads to work, I reetch out and taykes Devlins hand tyte in myne.

Thank you for the gruel, I says and he smyles at me. We skweeze each uvvers hands afore lettin go.

I WORKS HARD THAT MORNIN, THE BRUSES BOVVER ME BUT I BITES MY LIP AND GETS ON WI IT, BRAYNE WHIRLIN AWAY.

This ent the end o it. There will be contseekwences to what we have dun. What I have dun. I am shore o it.

At letters, Devlin and Thomas sit either side o me.

What are we to do Thomas? I says. He ent goin to let it rest is he, the Master I meen, wi Walsh gone when tis cleer they was workin on the sayme side and all.

But what if it ent just us? says Devlin sudden lyke. What if there are uvvers in Bearmouth tryin to stand up for thereselves eh? Men lyke Rickerbee see. Maybe the Master is less concernd bout us than you think.

We must be cayreful, says Thomas. We must keep our heads down and all will be well.

I catch Devlins eye and I can see hes thinkin sayme as me. All ent goin to be well. How can it possiblee be?

At mess we is proved ryte. Cos things all chaynge when Mr Sharp comes over to us.

We is moved, our whole dorm moved, and we is startin the next day. All o us moved to seams further away from the rolley roads. Awkwud men. Tis what we thawt myte be comin and here tis.

Why? says Thomas and Mr Sharp shrugs.

Tis the Masters orders, he says. Wants to go back and open up that part o the mine a bit more. Thinks you lot are the best fellas for it.

Really? says Jack growlin lyke. Best men and move em farther aways so tis harder for em to maykes a livin eh?

Mr Sharp shrugs again. Tis an honor to praps be openin up a new part o the mine, he says. You should be pleased.

Jack growls again lyke a dog and Mr Sharp knos to tayke his leeve.

I think again o what Devlin says. What if it ent just us askin questions, tryin to stand up for theirselves? I looks around the mess, looks at the fayces eatin their meet and tatties and I thinks which o em myte be in the sayme situayshun. Who else here is an awkwud man?

But the fayces all look the sayme. Grey and tired. Carnt always read a fayce lyke a book see.

IN DORM THAT EVE WE ARE ALL CAST DOWN ON OUR LUCK AND FEELIN RYTE SORRY FOR OURSELVES.

Leest we got rid o Walsh eh, says Jack candul lyte flickrin cross his fayce. Lookin on the bryte side an all.

Less coinage now tho, says Skillen and Nicholson nods. They looks at me.

Ent Newts fawlt, says Devlin firm lyke.

No. No it ent, says Thomas but none uvver do chip in.

We all sits in silence for a bit.

How many men been lost down here? I says thinkin out loud. We lost Gamble and Harrison and Tobe, I says.

And fore that Ellison and Harris and Carter, says Skillen.

And fore that Kwinn and Buddall, says Jack, if you remembers as far backs as I dos. Smyth and Bell and all.

And the severn that went in the xplosion, says Thomas.

And the youngs in the slip slide, I says.

In the last year alone I maykes it close to thirtee, says Thomas.

Tis a dayngeruss bisness so tis, says Jack. Always has been. Tis how it is. Atonin for our forefarvers eh, says so in the Maykers Prayer.

But Mr Johnson dunt seem to be atonin for nothin, I says. Seems to me he be proffitin from us all. And then hes openin our letters, spyin on us—what if he ent sendin our coinage home eh? What if hes just keepin it for hisself? What proof do we have eh? I says.

What proof do we have o the Mayker? says Jack. Tis how it is Newt.

Why tho? I says. Why do we just tayke things as they are see, why carnt we tryes to chaynge em?

We ent got the power to chaynge things, says Skillen. Thomas he tryes wi all his clever words to get a payrise and that ent workin so what else can we do, eh?

We have numbers, I says. Look around mess and how many fayces there are. And so many uvver levels too. More fayces, more men, more lads.

But we carnt meet up wi em, says Thomas. No gatherins sayve the number can fit in caban which is sayme as a dorm, up to a dozen men or lads. No more.

But we gathers in mess dunt we? I says. And we gathers in the Maykers Hall. All o us, the whole mine together.

What you sayin xactly Newt? says Nicholson, watchin me from the corner.

Are we all treeted the sayme? I says. Cos the men on the upper levels, tis cooler there and they wear more clothes so do they pays more for their clothes than us? Do they eat the sayme as us? Where are their mess halls cos they ent all fittin into ours eh? Is there, I swallows fore I says it, more than one Maykers Hall?

No Newt, no, says Jack firmly. No. It ent no good askin all these things. It dunt get you nowhere in the end dos it? All those words and talkin and stuff.

I didunt beat Walsh wi words or strength, I says. I beats him wi cleverness tis what.

And we is all bein punnishd for it now tho ent we? says Jack. And no I ent sayin tis yore fawlt Newt, cos twas me that ryled the fella I wunt denys it. But we must work twyce as hard now to be undun as awkwud men and for things to go back the way they was eh.

Will and Joe nods silently, Skillen too.

Nicholson eyes me.

What wud you have us do Newt? he says. Fyte wi our mandrils eh? Blow up the mine?

All I want is to be treeted fayre, I says. For all o us to be treeted fayre. Ent too much to ask tis it eh?

Tis the Maykers will, says Jack. We are awkwud men as penance for what happend to Walsh and we must atone throo our work. Ent no more to say on the subjekt. Let us pray, says Jack. In the beginnin there was the Mayker and he mayde all around us.

The uvvers join in. He mayde all the men and all the wimmin. He mayde all the creetures on this, his Earf.

I closes my eyes for a moment but when I looks back up Devlin ent joinin in neether. He looks at me, grim fayced until they say amen and Thomas blows out the lyte.

DEVLIN DUNT BELIEVE IN THE MAYKER. Im shore o it.

And I ent shore I believe in him myself no more neether.

But I am still afrayd to say it out loud so I says nothin. Ent none can read my thawts but still, they weighs hevvy on me.

AT GRUEL TIS CLEER TO ME THAT WE GET A LITTLE LESS THAN WE DID BEFORE AND IM SHORE TIS COS WE IS NOW LAYBELLD AWKWUD THO ENT NO ONE SAYIN IT.

We eats in silence.

Arfter, Devlin and I follow Jack and Skillen down to our new playce o work.

They sings as they heads down and we listerns as we follow em. Tis the first time I herd the words cleerly.

> *Jowl, jowl and listern lad*
> *Yule hear the coalfayce workin*
> *Theres many a marrer missin lad*
> *Becos he wuldnt listern lad*
> *Me farvver always used to say*
> *Pit works more than hewin*
> *You got to cokes the coal along*
> *And not be rivin and chewin*
> *The deputy crawls from flat to flat*
> *The putter rams the chummins*
> *And the man at the fayce must kna his playce*
> *Lyke a muvver knas her young un*

Must kna his playce, says Devlin. Tis what Jack thinks eh?

Maybe hes ryte, I says. Maybe tis just how things are is all.

You believe that? he says.

Dunt kno, I says. Dunt kno rytely what I believes no more.

I got to get out o here Newt, he says clutchin at my arm. I carnt stand it down here. Tis lyke workin in the very pits o hell. The darkness crushin yore spirits, feelin hungree all the time and feelin so tired that tis as much as I can do to rowse myself up out o bed. It ent ryte that we are here, he says. It ent ryte. We wunt born to live lyke moles in the dark. We are creetures o daylyte and green, creetures o blue skyes.

Praps yore ryte, I says. But we carnt just walk out o here, costs thirtee for the lift sharft and I ent got anywhere near that much. And then what, back to Ma and livin in one room and I ent able to pay my way? I says.

There must be anuvver way, he says.

Maybe there is, I says, but we got to find it then ent we?

And find it fast, he says lookin at me. Afore I loses my mind.

And afore I turn more wimminly than can be hidden, I thinks but I keeps that thawt firmly to myself.

TIS HARDER WORK IN THIS PART O THE MINE, FURTHER TO GET TO IN THE FIRST PLAYCE AND THEN HARDER TO BRING THE COAL UP TO THE ROLLEY ROAD. There ent no rails in this part o the mine and tis too unsteddy underfoot for ponys so all has to be dun by hand. Tis fayre the most nackerd I ever been to tell the trooth.

We must needs find anuvver playce for learnin letters too as our old playce is too far aways to get to now.

When I opens the payper to find my crust to eat durin letters I spyes mold on it, green dust lyke, and Thomas says it ent good for a body to eat such things so I maykes do wi nibblin round the edges lyke a mouse.

I keeps thinkin about him comin up at me from behind, I says quietly. Walsh. Wonderin if twill happen again lyke wi anuvver man. Wonderin whats next. But I realized somethin else too. I been livin in fear the whole time anyways. Even thinkin that tis the Maykers way, all them deaths, we taykes it for granted but it ent ryte is it? It ent ryte to live in fear evryday.

I thinks for a moment. That time when you says it only taykes one person to start a revolushun Devlin, it ent troo, I says. It taykes a whole army o people, it taykes numbers. Theres just three o us and if we carnt even get Jack to listern to us we ent got no hope convincin anyone else.

Dunt be despondent, says Thomas. We may not have numbers but we do have uvver things, he says.

147

How? I says. Where? What uvver things?

Thomas looks down at his hands. We got hands, he says. We got braynes. We got mandrils for diggin coal. And best o all we got this, he says and he smyles as he holds up a stick o dynamyte.

Turns out for all o Thomass learnedness he is also a theevin barstard and I loves him even more for it.

Hes been theevin dynamyte and fuses for some time now, hydin it under Harrisons bed twixt aynchunt mattress and bedsted. Just a stick now and then but tis a few sticks he dos have now.

Tis a tricky thing dynamyte, says Thomas. You must respekt her.

He tells us how to use it, drillin a hole first usin a hand drill and then very cayrefullee settin the dynamyte in. You sets the charge and then you runs swiftlee to a sayfe playce and then boom. Tis dun.

But it ent that simple o corse. He has told me such things before and I kno tis all sorts o uvver things to consider and all, manner o the rock, where you drill the hole, how long the fuse should be, you got to kno all these things see and that dos tayke xpeerients and me and Devlin we ent got that.

Thomas tells us that we ent to use it or touch it or tell anyone else about it for now. Not even Jack and the uvvers in the dorm. Tis somethin we must keep among ourselves.

Tis strayngely comfortin to kno that we have got force if we need it tho. I feel lyke when Thomas give me the nyfe that I still got in my pockit, sayfer just knowin I has it on me. Cayse o the lykes o Walsh.

AT MESS WE ARE FAYRE WORN OUT BUT WE ALL NOTISSES SOMETHIN NEW. A large blackbord is nayled onto the wall. In white at the top it dos say Your Efforts Have Produced and then underneeth that there is two lynes see, collums Thomas calls em. The left one says Last Week and the ryte one says This Week and then numbers is chalked on, the amount in tons we dug up o coal.

When we is all sittin and eatin Mr Sharp comes in and blows a whissul loud lyke. We stops eatin and looks at him.

Yule notiss the new bord, he says. Tis the Masters orders so as you can see what we is producin at the moment. Cos produktivitee has gone downwud, he says. And that ent no good for anyone as meens yule get payd less and we got less coal to sell see.

He wypes his nose and in trooth I thinks to myself I never did see a man wi more o a runny nose than him.

The Master wants you to see what you is producin, he says. And this weeks got to be better than last weeks and next weeks better than this weeks see.

I looks around at mess and I sees emptee seats. Tobes. Walshs. Ent neether o them been filld. And I looks around further and there is more emptee seats. And it strykes me that there ent been replaycements for those that have gone. So Mr Sharp is askin the impossible see cos tis not ryte that a man can carry on diggin out more and more when there ent enuff hands to do it eh.

Ent none says anythin about the bord, but you can feel

folk ent happy bout it. But Mr Sharp knos this so he says those who do best at haulin the coal will earn xtra rashuns as well as coinage and the room dos chaynge instunt lyke.

The best team will win free beer on paydays, he says, as much as they can drink.

And the whole room dos cheer him, bang bangin on taybles and the lyke. Mr Sharp looks round the room ryte pleased at his work and I catch his eye and he just smyle smyles.

I feels lyke standin up and sayin tis just a con, tis just a con but ent none listernin to a young. And I knos twill mayke things harder for us. We ent goin to be gettin more and more coal out o our patch cos tis too long a seam and we is at the bottom end o it. No free beer for any o our dorm.

And I see Nicholsons eyes on me strayte from the uvver side o the bentch and I kno he has clockd the sayme thing and I dunt feel so comftable arfter all. Cos I can sees now that this is how they rid themselves o the awkwudest one see, by forcin em out. By leevin em wi no frends, by maykin their own fellas turn on em.

THERE ENT NO TALKIN TO JACK AND THE UVVERS, THEY ALL THINK THE ONLY WAY FORWUDS IS TO WORK AS HARD AS A BODY CAN. They think tis the only way they can undo bein awkwud men but I ent so shore about that.

I lies in bed that nyte churn churnin things over in my head and there tis. Suddenlee. An idea. Lyke a lyte itself bryte as lectrick. Tis a risk and I realize too that I carnt do it by myself but tis an idea and a good one at that. But I got to be cayreful, tis an idea that many will find hard to stomarck and I must needs think it throo fore I shares it wi anyone, even Thomas and Devlin.

I have nyte trubbles again wi Walsh reetchin for me out o the darkness and hands wandrin over me. I wayke in a sweat panic panickin wi my heart raycin away. Tis a while afore I dare goes back to sleep again but come the mornin I am resolvd.

I undun Walsh wi cleverness and so tis that I must use it elsewhere and all.

AS THINGS NORMALLY STAND, WE HEADS TO THE PUMPS STRAYTE ARFTER SHIFTS BUT SINCE STARTIN THE MONTHLEES, I TRYES TO HEAD BACK TO THE DORM FIRST TO CHECK THAT IT ENT COME BACK. Thomas did say it can be unprediktaball sometimes so tis best I am caushuss.

When I turns up, the panel is harf pushed over the entry so I peeks my head round to see Nicholson rummidgin throo the uvvers beds. I think o Thomass dynamyte hidden under Harrisons bed and sos I pushs the panel open and steps strayte in, hand on my nyfe.

What you doin Nicholson? I says, voyce steddy as I can hold it.

He looks at me, cawt in the act and dunt kno where ryte to look.

What you doin? I says again.

Could ask sayme o you, he says.

I left somethin here. What you left here eh? I says.

Nicholson ent shore how much I seen, so tis cleer hes tryin to think o somethin to say.

Left somethin underneeth Devlins bed eh? I says. I taykes out my nyfe and holds it in front o me. Dunt think I wunt use it, I says. Altho trooth be told I ent got the stomarck for anuvver fyte, I thinks to myself.

Nicholsons fayce dos crumble lyke poor qualitee coal.

I ent meenin no harm, he says. I ent meenin no harm. He puts his hands up lyke surrendrin in a fyte.

Spyin on us eh? I says jab jabbin the nyfe towards him.

He sits down on Tobes emptee bunk and puts his head
in his hands.

I dunt meen to Newt, he says. But tis hard to mayke ends
meet and they offerd me ten more coins a week to do it.

Who did? I says, but I alreddy knos the answer.

Mr Sharp, he says snifflin away. I dunt meen to Newt,
I kno tis wrong, I kno it see but I carnt be an awkwud man
eh, I dunt do nothin wrong.

How long you been spyin on us? I ask.

Since arfter Walsh went, he says.

You dunt told em bout that then at leest.

I ent a bad man Newt I ent, he says. Not lyke Walsh, he
was a wrong un and you did ryte to finish him off. I mayde a
promiss not to tell bout that so I dunt.

Praps, I says. Nyfe still in hand. Poyntin towards
him. Or maybe you thawt it implikaytd you and all. Dob
the whole dorm in and you the only one left eh? None
in the whole o Bearmouth wuld work wi you arfter that.
Untrustworthee youd be deemd eh?

That ent it, he says. I swear Newt, I ent a bad man.
I dunt brayke my promisses. Not ever.

Why dunt you proov you ent a bad man eh? I says,
holdin the nyfe out.

How? he says.

Mayke stuff up and feed that back to Mr Sharp, I says.

Lyin, he says, that what you meen?

Corse, I says. You still get that xtra coinage and the rest
o the dorm dunt need to kno.

But what can I say? he says. Mayker sayve us lyin tis
a sin.

Lyin can be the trooth, I says. Just a diffrent vershun
o it. Lyke Jack wants to go back ryte, all o us do, we ent

awkwud men are we, none o us? So tell em there plan has workd, I says. One more week o bein awkwud men and that should skwish skwash any thawts o bad things there ever was. And you collect a week and a harfs xtra coinage and no I dunt want none, I says, keeps it all to yourself you can.

And you wunt tell the uvvers? he says.

No, I says. I promiss. But I want you to promiss somethin to me and all. Seein as youre a fella that dos never brayke a promiss.

Anythin, he says.

If you ever spyes on us properlee, if you ever lies to us, your only frends down here, I will tell all the uvvers and then I ent goin to be the only one comin for you then see, I says.

No, he says.

So no spyin on us ever again. Promiss and shayke on it, I says and I spits and holds out my hand.

Will you put the nyfe away? he says.

No, I says. Not til you shayke.

He comes forwuds, wary lyke and then offers his hand spittin on it first.

Go on, I says.

And he shaykes. I promiss, he says.

See you at mess, I says, lettin his hand drop and he nods.

As he sneeks out past the panel he turns to me.

Youve chaynged Newt, he says. Youve chaynged ent you?

I grew up tis what, I says to him. I ent no baby no more tis all.

He nods his head at me and then leeves.

I sit down on my bed heart thumpin away and I lets out a deep breath.

That ent a bad job Newt, I says to myself in my head lyke. That ent a bad job at all.

Cos if Mr Sharp and the Master run this playce by cleverness and mannipewlayshun stands to reeson that a body wi a bit o brayne can do the sayme.

When Im reddy, I check under Harrisons bed to see if Thomass dynamyte is still there and it is, hidden in the old springs but tis there. I counts em, three sticks in total. I dunt believe Nicholson wuld think to look there but I moves it all just in cayse. Wi my nyfe I cuts a hole in Tobes old mattress and pushs em in nyce and tyte.

None will find em there, I thinks to myself. A small victoree Newt, I thinks and I smyles to myself, but a victoree neverless.

I ENT IMAGININ IT ARFTER ALL BUT TIS CLEER THAT WE ARE GETTIN LESS FOOD AT MESS. The meet and tatties we get is smaller porshuns alryte. I looks at Nicholson and he looks strayte back at me.

Well it ent goin to be forever now is it? I says tryin to be cheerful. We is all workin hard as we can so carnt be long fore Mr Sharp brings us back to the fold, I says.

Corse, says Nicholson eyin me. It carnt be long eh.

Jack and Skillen nod but Devlin looks at me straynge lyke.

What you up to Newt? he whispers to me as we head back to dorm.

Nothin in partickular, I says. Nothin.

THOMAS, DO YOU BELIEVE IN THE MAYKER? I SAYS TO HIM NEXT DAY AT LETTERS.

What? he says lyke he ent believin his own ears for a moment.

Do you believe in the Mayker? I says.

Corse, he says. Dunt we all believe in the Mayker?

Yes, I says. But do you <u>really</u> believe in him?

Thomas sits there in silence for a moment.

I dunt believe in him, says Devlin arfter a while.

Thomas shaykes his head, disapproovin lyke.

Why? I says.

Cos Pa tort me that not evryone believes the sayme thing, Devlin says. There are uvver gods, uvver beliefs all over. Imagine that.

Uvver gods? I says and Devlin nods.

Uvver gods. Lyke uvver storyes that Thomas and you mayke up.

Ah, says Thomas. But not all storyes are real.

But you do believe in him, the Mayker, Thomas? I says and he nods.

Tis all I kno, he says. The Mayker is wi us wherere we are.

Do you really think that? I says.

I hope it is so, he says. Ent that all we can do?

It ent a full answer from him but tis enuff for me to kno that my plan carnt inclood him. Needs must be me and Devlin.

Arfter letters we walks back down the rolley road

together candul lit as Devlin still ent no good in the dark. Tis a trooly emptee part o the mine that we are in as awkwud men and so tis the perfect playce to ask him. I grabs his arm.

What? he says as he turns to fayce me and I put my finger on his lips for a moment.

The Mayker, I whispers. Tis sed he will give us a sine ryte, in the Maykers Prayer. Tis a sine that he gives and then we wil rise up from undergrawnd. Tis the words o the prayer.

So, says Devlin. So what?

Well if the Mayker ent real, there ent never goin to be no sine ryte? I says.

Alryte, says Devlin.

So if there ent ever goin to be no sine, maybe tis best we mayke one o our own eh, I says.

His eyes wyden as the idea sinks into his brayne.

You meen?

Yes, I says. And I thawt o the very thing. But I need to kno if you can be trustd.

He nods and looks hurt. Corse I can Newt, he says. Carnt believe you askd.

I smyles at him.

Needed to hear you say it is all, I says. You carnt tell no one else about it neether, I says. Not even Thomas.

And he nods.

Promiss? I says and he nods again. Got to say it, I says. Out loud.

So he dos. I promiss, he says. He holds out his hand and we shaykes on it.

Alryte, he says. Come on then brayve little Newt. What is this plan o yours then? he says.

And I taps my nose and winks at him.

All in good time, I says, all in good time.

On the way back to Jack I see a teeny patch o some green gold lichen. Trooth be told I ent shore how it can survive down here but I touch it for good luck. I feels the softness under my fingers and more than anythin it feels lyke hope.

AT MESS, WE EAT OUR MEET AND TATTIES AS SLOW AS WE CAN.
Eke ekin out our meeslee porshuns.

We are all too tired to talk much and I realize that tis anuvver advantidge o callin a man awkwud, he is too tired to plot or plan arfter shifts. I says so, and I sees Nicholson nod at me.

Maykers Day tomorro, says Thomas. We must pray that we are not awkwud men for long now.

Amen to that, says Jack. Amen.

And I say nothin.

THE NEXT DAY, AS WE GO UP AND UP TO THE MAYKERS HALL, IT ENT THE LEVELS IM A COUNTIN ON MY FINGERS. Tis the number o guards we goes past insted.

As we chants the Maykers Prayer, my maw dos open and shut lyke a trapdoor but the words dunt meen nothin to me.

I askd the Mayker for a sine but none was forthcomin.

I askd him to show hisself to me. I askd for him to listern.

I askd him how he could let Walsh do that to Tobe.

I askd him why we wayte for a better life in the next life when shorely we should be livin now too.

I askd him so much and I ent herd nothin.

I wayte for a punnishment, for the Mayker to curse me for havin killd a man but there ent nothin.

I skwints and looks up at the Maykers fayce, but all I see is rock.

Mayker forgive me, I says to myself in my head.

And I think heethenish thawts so I do.

Mayker help me, I says.

But the words, they is just letters, lyke sayin the alphabet all throo. Just words words words.

THE NEXT DAY, THOMAS FAYRE GRABS ME WHEN I ARRIVE AT LETTERS AND SHAYKES ME BY THE SHOLDERS. Devlin puts an arm on him to stop.

What what? I says and Thomas lets me go.

Who did you tell about the dynamyte eh? he whispers, fury buildin in him. Did you say anythin? he says to Devlin.

I moved it, I says, from Harrisons bed to Tobes. Ent none goin to look for it there eh.

Mayker protekt us. Why Newt, he says, why move it at all?

And I fayce the choyce o grassin up Nicholson and tellin the trooth or lyin. But whats one lie more now? I thinks.

Cayse o spyes is what, I says. Cos the Master offerd me coinage for spyin so whos to say he ent offerd someone else the sayme eh, I says.

You should o askd me, he says, growlin.

Im sorry Thomas, I says in the smallest voyce I can muster and he nods.

I thawt I had been discoverd, he says. That we were undun.

Im sorry Thomas, I says. I was thinkin o sayfe guardin all o us see.

Alryte, he says. Tis alryte. But you must never do it again.

I nod. Corse, I says. Sorry.

He ruffles my hair. Tis alryte Newt. But you must ask permishun eh. If we carnt trust each uvver in the dorm, who can we trust?

I nods. I kno, I says. Thinkin o how close Nicholson myte o come to xposin us and how we carnt trust anyone at all.

But tho Thomas believes in the Mayker wi blind fayth lyke, he is also the most learned man I kno and altho I think the plan to creayte a sine is a good one, as dos Devlin, I do so want to ask Thomas about it.

I resist and resist but I carnt stop myself. I tells him about creatin a sine ourselvs, layter on when tis just the three o us.

Thomas is not angry wi us. Tis far wurse, he is disappoyntd.

Tis heethenish, Thomas says. The Mayker will see your thawts, tis a terriball thing to do. If you were to get cawt or tell anyone else you wuld get most severely punnishd for it. Mayker protekt us, what were you thinkin? he says, sadness in his eyes. And how did you think to creayte a sine? he asks.

Praps wi some o your dynamyte, I whispers, lookin at the ground. A bang or an xplosion or the lyke.

You myte o killd yourselves, Thomas says. And for what?

For the chance to allow men to escaype and to free them, says Devlin.

Tis heethenish, says Thomas.

Tis a way out, I says. Besides, why was you puttin the dynamyte to one side eh?

Tis diffrent, says Thomas. Tis for emergencies, cayse we need to fyte back.

This is fytin back, I says. Tis xactly that.

Thomas shaykes his head. Tis a last resort Newt, tis what it is. When all talkin is dun and there ent no more to say.

You dint get too far wi the Master wi talkin, I says but Thomas dunt agree.

I will tayke the dynamyte back myself, he says. And hide it somewhere else.

No, I says. I wunt tayke it wi out askin, tis why I told you about the plan see. Cos I needed your blessin.

Well you carnt have it, he says. Im sorry Newt but tis a step too far and you ent knowin xactly what youre doin wi it. No. I will hide the dynamyte, he says. Somewhere else.

WHEN IM ALONE WI DEVLIN ON OUR WAY BACK TO WORK, HE IS FAYRE ANGRY WI ME FOR TELLIN THOMAS ABOUT THE SINE.

I wantd his blessin, I says. Tis all. He dunt want us to do it and fayres fayre but that dunt meen we ent goin to do it see. Tis just I wuld have lyked him to help us. It dunt matter anyways, I says. We ent goin to have the energy to put any proper plan together til arfter we are back in our old playce in the mine. And we myte o thawt o somethin else by then.

What if that dunt happen tho? says Devlin. What happens if we ent tayken back?

One more week, I says thinkin o Nicholson. And if not, we go ahead wi somethin anyways.

It dunt even tayke one more week tho as the next day at mess arfter work on the Tewsday, Mr Sharp tells us that we are to be moved back to the mine proper from the next Munday.

You ent producin the amounts that the Master wants down there so we is movin you back, he says, sniffin at us. The Master wants to close down that part o the mine arfter all, tis cleer to him now that the coal be mostly gone from there see.

And thats that. Just a few words from Mr Sharp and we is back to where we were.

Fore more days then, says Jack. Fore more days is all, then tis Maykers Day and we is all back to where we was. See Newt, he says, work hard and tis rewarded. Tis a lessun for you too Devlin, all this talk o nonsense. See, what gets us back in the good books is towin the lyne and workin as hard as we can.

Devlin nods lyke hes listernin.

Corse Jack, he says. You been here the longest so you got more years on us.

Devlin catches my eyes and smyles at me and I feels all warm inside.

New start on Munday, Devlin says and I nods at him.

New start, I says.

TIS OUR LAST DAY AS AWKWUD MEN WHEN THE AXIDENT HAPPENS. The xplosion fayre goes throo me and Jack as I fills up the basket wi the coal hes chippin out. The roof o the mine shudders and judders above us and bits o rock fall down on us. We croutch low, fayces down, holdin our heads til it settles.

Mayker sayve us, says Jack. What in Maykers nayme was that?

But Im alreddy runnin see, runnin runnin up to the rolley road. Cos I kno Thomas and Nicholson ent plannin no xplosions this mornin.

I ent shore quite where they is in the mine so I stops for a moment to get my breath back, but I see lytes flick flickrin down in the distance down to the far left and I hears Nicholson shoutin for help.

Help help, he says and tis gettin louder when I sees him runnin towards me. Eyes white, wyde open, blood runnin down one blacknd cheek.

We needs the stretcher, we needs the stretcher, he says. Tis Thomas, Newt, tis Thomas.

I ent hearin else more then as I pushs past Nicholson and runs back down in the direkshun he cayme from.

I dunt see Thomas at first, tis a wall o coal I come to wi a small candul flick flickrin off the wall and then I sees him, harf trappd in the wall, crushd by a support beam cross his middle, pinnin him down to the ground.

Thomas, I says. Thomas.

I runs to him, croutchin by him, and I listerns quietly but his breath is all raggd and tis cleer that he dos find it paynful to talk.

Thomas, I says. Tis alryte. Nicholson is gettin the stretcher, twill be fast as anythin and we will get help and—

He dunt let me finish tho.

Newt, he says, crokin lyke. Newt listern to me. Tis important.

Im listernin, I says. Im listernin I promiss Thomas.

I ent maykin it out o here.

I skweeze his hand.

You will Thomas you will. Tis but a moment and the stretcher will be here and—

No Newt, he says. Let me say what I must.

I wypes my eyes but my tears drip drip onto his sleeve.

He holds my hand tyte.

You must get out o here, he says. Start a new life far away. Please Newt promiss me.

I will try, I says. I will, I promiss but tis alryte Thomas you will come too.

No Newt, he says. I carnt be comin wi you. The Mayker is comin for me see.

He strokes my fayce, cuppin my cheek in his warm hand.

Thomas, I says sniffin. Thomas dunt leeve me.

The dynamyte is still under Tobes bed where you hid it, he whispers. I ent moved it. You needs must do what you feel is ryte. He holds my hand tyte. I will always be in your heart, he says slowly lyke as if he is strugglin to stay awayke.

I sob and sob and kiss his hand and hold it so so tyte close to me.

He turns his eyes to look at the candul flick flickrin.

Look Newt, he whispers, tis just lyke a star in the nyte sky.

The candul flick flickers and then Thomas dos give a large sigh as if the wayte o the world was lifted off o him and I see from his eyes that the spark has gone out o him.

Thomas? I says but he ent hearin nothin no more.

The lyte flickers and then the candul gives a last puff o smoke fore goin out too.

I sits there in the dark, hand held tyte tytely around Thomass til I hears Nicholsons footsteps behind me wi Devlin and Jack.

Tis too layte, I says sniffin lyke. Tis too layte. He is gone.

ALL IS LOST.

I am undun.

Thomas is dead.

I close my eyes and I sees it all again.

A new candul lit and the fayces o the men around me. Nicholson and Skillen, Jack and Devlin. The twins.

We shovels the coal away from Thomas so we can pull him out. It taykes most all o us to hold the beam up so Jack can drag his body out.

As Jack and Nicholson lift him into the stretcher, a long wooden box shayped lyke a coffin alreddy, tis cleer that Thomass lower harf was fayre crushd underneeth the beam and the wayte o coal.

Tis the Maykers way, says Jack as he puts a hand on my sholder. Tis the Maykers way Newt and he is wi him now so he is.

Devlin puts his arm round my sholders and holds me tyte.

There ent nothin we could o dun, says Jack. He was gone when we got here eh.

Nicholson, who I ent ever seen upset afore, goes to his nees by the stretcher and taykes Thomass hand.

Tis my fawlt, he says. We was drillin holes for the dynamyte for this arfternoon, close this part down for good see. I was hungree lyke and sed Id brayke for lunch early but Thomas keeps on workin on his own. Twas a rockfall I think. I hears him shout to me, here Nicholson, come have a look and then hes shoutin, run run, and I is runnin and

170

when I look he ent behind me and then the xplosion fayre pushs me out. And I runs back and there he is. There he is.

Tis the Maykers way, says Jack pattin Nicholson on the back. Tis the Maykers way.

Rockfall must o set off the dynamyte at the sharft end, says Nicholson his hands shaykin still. I am ryte sorry for it, he says, wypin his fayce. I am ryte sorry for it Thomas.

In the beginnin there was the Mayker and he mayde all around us, says Jack.

> *He mayde all the men and all the wimmin*
> *He mayde all the creetures on this, his Earf*
> *The Mayker loved each and evryone o us*
> *But then all us men and wimmin betrayd him*
> *They took his Trust and spatt on it*
> *And the Mayker was angry*
> *He sent us down into the dark Earf*
> *To atone for the sins o our forefarvers and muvvers*

And one day, tis sed, the Mayker will give us a sine, says Jack and I look at Devlin and he looks at me and I nods at him and he nods back.

> *We will all be foregivven*
> *And we will rise up to the land*
> *And the lyte that the Mayker holds there in his parm*
> *Will be givern to all o us*
> *And all shall prosper in this life and the next.*

Amen, we all says.

Amen.

I CARNT BELIEVE HE IS GONE. I keep turnin as if he is behind me, I keep hearin his voyce in my head. I feels him all around me still and yet.

And yet.

He is gone. Thomas gone. Tobe too. Both gone.

And my heart dos brayke all over again.

TIS LYKE A BLACK CLOUD DOS SURROUND ME PINNIN ME DOWN.

I dunt want to move, dunt want to do nothin cept hide.

Tis as much as I can do to sup some water.

Pinin is what Jack calls it. He says Thomas is wi the Mayker now and I should tayke comfort in that but I carnt.

Cos the Mayker taykes evryone dear to me.

Tis his way, tis his way, says Jack again and again. Tis his way.

Devlin sits alone wi me in dorm.

Carnt believe hes gone, he says and I nod.

How many more must he tayke? I says. How many more?

We must do what we sed, says Devlin. The sine.

I carnt, I says. What if this is punnishment from the Mayker for thinkin heethenish thawts?

But it ent tho, says Devlin. What about the uvver men who died, the uvver boys eh? They was tayken long afore you started questionin things. Bearmouth tis full o daynger and horrors. And lest we chaynge things, ent goin to be no chaynge forever.

I ent reddy yet, I says. Not now.

When then? says Devlin.

Soon I says. But I carnt answer for shore. My despayre dos wrap around me lyke a blanket.

ON MAYKERS DAY, MR SHARP LEADS A SPESHUL PRAYER FOR THOMAS. I ent listernin to him trooth be told as it hurts too much to think o not seein Thomas again, not hearin his voyce. No more letters, no more learnedness. He is gone. Thomas is gone.

The Mayker has ordayned it and it was to be so, says Mr Sharp dronin on.

Amen, all around us do say.

A wave o sadness washes over me and tis all I can do to keep myself standin up. I feel Devlin at my elbow, holdin my arm.

I look up at the Maykers fayce but tis all just rocks now.

I want to shayke those around me. I want to shout and poynt to the rocks, see, see, there ent no Mayker here. Tis just rocks sayme as you see evryday.

But I carnt. I must look and act lyke a believer. Act and look and hide the deceever that I am. And yet my heart feels hollower than ever.

ARFTER PRAYERS JACK INVITES ME AND DEVLIN TO CABAN FOR THE FIRST TIME. Tis an honour to be askd, shows we are thawt o as men now. Men. Feels funny sayin that when I ent nothin lyke a man but I keeps my trap shut tyte. Tis my seekret now, myne alone now that Thomas ent here. I dunt want to sit in caban and sing and talk. I want to distrakt myself else thawts o Thomas do crowd into my brayne and over whelm my very head.

Insted, I taykes Devlin to see the ponys. I promisd him a few days past we wuld go to celebrayte not bein awkwud men no more and I keeps my promisses.

I ent quite shore o the way wi out Thomas so we gets a bit lost trooth be told, even wi Devlins candul lytin the way. All the men are at caban and we hears singin in the distance as we wanders around the sharfts and tunnels.

We ent lost are we? says Devlin and I shaykes my head.

Corse we ent lost, I says sharp lyke.

We carryes on for a moment til Devlin stops sudden.

Wayte, he says. And I stop too.

What? I says. What is it?

The candul lyte flick flickers lyke it dos sometimes wi the straynge breezes and drafts that you do get undergrawnd. It ent chayngin color or nothin tho so we are cleer o daynger o the lykes o arfterdamp.

What? I says.

Smell, he says. Smell.

175

I lifts my nose up and I sniff sniff but I carnt smell nothin.

What? I says.

Carnt you smell it a bit? he says.

I sniffs and tryes but there ent nothin. Just the dampness o Bearmouth lyke always.

Maybe I imagind it, he says sadly and we stay stock still for a moment.

No, there it is, he says, feverd happy lyke.

All I can smell is a faynte onyons smell lyke armpits or somethin.

Thats it, he says. Dunt you kno what it is?

No, I says. Cos it ent armpits is it?

Tis wild garlick, he says. Im shore o it.

A plarnt? Ent no plarnt grows at these depths dos it? I says.

No, he says. But praps it meens somethin. Praps it meens that we have tunneld so far under the earf that we are a comin out somewhere else, he says.

His joy tis fayre playne to see.

Dunt be darft, I says. We been headin down ent we, not up.

But what if down leads us out? he says. Lyke a mountin tis lyke a pyramyd so if you starts harfways up on one side and goes down and down and out, where myte you end up eh?

At the ground on the uvver side, I says.

Xactly, he says.

I go to sniff again but the smell is gone. The candul flickers.

Tis spring, he says. Tis spring and the wild garlick is in flower.

176

I carnt smell it no more, I says. Praps tis nowt but our maginins.

Praps, he says. But praps tis a bit o hope too eh.

We stand there sniff sniffin but there ent nothin sayve candul flaymes and dampness.

Come on, I says at last, we ent got all day.

But afore we heads off, Devlin taykes out a bit o chalk from his pockit and he dos draw, small lyke, a flower that looks lyke a ball o petals on one o the wooden support beams holdin up the roof.

Tis wild garlick, he says. Dunt you kno what it looks lyke?

I shaykes my head.

Ent never seen it I reckons. Ent never smelld it neether but if that was it and it dos smell lyke armpits o men I dunt think tis a grayte loss to have not sniffd it afore, I says.

He larfs and tis a rare thing to hear. It dos mayke me feel warm inside. Then I remember Thomas again and the numbness returns.

Tis hope, Devlin says. Tis hope. Come on then, he says. Lead on.

DEVLIN IS GOOD WI THE PONYS. They lykes him they do, tis cleer to see. Boy dos remark on it as he watches em.

Mayjor sniffs and nuzzalls me and tis an odd thing but it feels lyke he sees I am sad, that he understands my loss.

Tis wrong to keep animals undergrawnd, says Devlin as he strokes Stars mane.

Boy shrugs. Ent no diffrent to keepin us down here, tis what I always says to Newt. We ent goin to be down here forever anyways, says Boy and we looks at him.

How so? I says.

The Masters movin us out, the ponys see. Sposed to be goin to anuvver mine but we ent.

Whys he movin the ponys? says Devlin.

Needed elsewhere is all, says Boy. But the men are stayin. Ent shore I should tell nobody so best keep quiet about it eh.

But what about the work? I says. Wunt the ponys be missd?

Boy shrugs. If you ask me this mines days are numberd. Bearmouth ent goin to be a never endin pit eh. Reckon tis a last push to get as much out as they can afore closin it down.

I remembers then the Master sayin about lecktrik, about not bringin it down to the deeps if the coal was to run dry and my mind is a whirlin.

You say you ent goin, Devlin says. What you goin to do Boy?

Boy grins. We be leavin the mine shore, he says, but

we ent goin down anuvver one. See I been sayvin all this time and I got enuff to get by and purchayse one or two o the ponys see. Ill find work somewhere else, on a farm or summat. Folk always need strong ponys to do work. Bit o fresh air and rest for em and they will be ryte as rain.

When do you go? I says and Boy shrugs.

Tis a waytin game now, he says. Im just waytin for when they taykes us back up and I ent never comin back down any pit anywheres so long as I live. He grins and one o his teeth is missin. Twill be sorry for those left behind, the lykes o you lot, he says, but I reckons your time will come soon enuff eh?

Devlin looks at me. I reckons so too, he says.

ON THE WAY BACK, DEVLIN IS SO FULL O THAWTS THAT HE FAYRE BOUNCES ALONG THE WALLS.

Tomorro is back to work, I says.

But back to work not as awkwud men, he says, not so far aways. When do we do the sine?

I puts my finger to my lips.

Ent no body here Newt, he larfs.

Carnt be too cayreful, I says.

So, he whispers. When?

Soon, I says.

Twill be dayngeruss, he whispers. What youre plannin?

What we are plannin, I says. Not me.

Twas your idea tho eh? he says.

If you dunt want to help you dunt have to, I says.

I do, he says. And I will and all. But we should stryke soon. If they are thinkin o closin Bearmouth, they will cayre even less about us. More axidents, more daynger. We need to act soon, he says.

Thing is, I says. I been thinkin about it and I ent shore our plan will work see. If we do blasts a hole in the layke ryte, emptee it out whilst men are at pumps, tis a huge sine shore but what if they all see it as an axident? What if in its sted, all the waters are drayned and all that happens is that we ent got clene water? Twill mayke things wurse for us all. It ent the ryte idea, tis all.

Devlin nods.

Alryte, he says. So we think o somethin better, he says. Somethin bigger, somethin better.

What? I says. Lyke what?

He shrugs. Somethin bigger. Somethin better. Yule think o somethin. You always do.

I CARNT EAT AT MESS. Jack beraytes me for it.

Thomas wunt want you to fayde away eh Newt? Tis the Maykers way that he has gone. He has gone to a better playce now and so there ent no poynte mopin see, he says sloppin and shovellin the food into his open maw and talkin as he dos so.

It dunt mayke no diffrence tho. Words dunt mayke you hungree. Words dunt mayke you forget.

I keeps seein him in the dark. Thomas. When my eyes are closed. I blinks and I sees him. But not as he was, strong and tall and wyse, but as a crushd harf man weighed down by deep dark rocks.

Devlin says this will chaynge. That twill fayde in time and I will remember him as he properlee was. As a learned man, as a kind man, as the farver I never had.

The only thing that gives me comfort is those words o his, o Thomass. That he is forever in my heart. Sometimes I put my hands to my heart and hold em there. Thinkin o him see and hopin that he is there.

Devlin says I must focus on the matter at hand but he dunt kno Thomas all his life see.

For me I fear losin him is too grayte to bear.

I am broke beyond repayre.

I DREAM O HIM.

I dream o clouds white and fluffee.

I dream o blue skyes and sunshyne.

I dream o clene water so bryte that your own reflekshun dos look lyke a shiny mirror.

I dream o green fields full o cattal and sheep.

I dream o a house, a small holdin lyke. A pond in the front wi ducks on it kwakk kwakkin and some hens peck peckin around the front door.

Tis red brick this house. And grey smoke dos weeve its way out o the chimnee.

I walks up the path towards the house, thinkin o the gingerbred house in Thomass storyes and when I get to the door he opens it. Thomas. Smylin and larfin he picks me up and holds me, whirlin me round and round.

I thawt youd gone forever, I cryes and he wypes my tears away.

Corse not, he says. Im always here see. And he taps my chest. Told you eh, always here.

We sits down in the kitchen and there is a feest awaytin us. Chees and bred and meets roastd and sweete wi there own juces. Ripe crunchee apples and pears, bryte red cherrys all piled up in heeps. There is waterd beer too and we drinks and eats and larfs.

Devlin lookin arfter you? he says and I larf.

Dunt need nobody to look arfter me, I says wi a mouth full o food and Thomas grins.

You lookin arfter Devlin then? he says and I nods.

Corse, I says.

Can I come and live here wi you? I says and he shaykes his head.

Tis too early for you. You must get out o Bearmouth first eh.

I looks around me at the walls o the cottage, the bricks and morta so real to me. The food I eat so real.

I will always be wi you, he says.

Help me Thomas, I says and the walls o the playce they start slip slidin away from me further and further.

I reetch out my arms and Thomas is still there but I carnt quite hold him and he is standin there, gettin bigger and bigger til he dos tower above me. A giant in front o me and then lyte comes from his eyes and out his fingers and out o all o him. Shinin bryte, so bryte that tis fayre blindin.

Tis a sine, I says. Tis a sine from the Mayker.

And Thomas reetches down to me and offers me his hand but tis so massiv and so bryte I almost screem.

I am always wi you, he says.

And tho I carnt see beyond the bryteness, I kno he is smylin.

I waykes up in a sweat. Tangld sheets and heat drippin.

I lie still waytin for my breethin to get back to normal.

Thank you, Thomas, I says to him in my head. Thank you.

For he has givern me an idea.

HOW WELL DO YOU CLIMB? I SAYS TO DEVLIN ON THE WAY TO GRUEL ON MUNDAY AND HE LOOKS AT ME FUNNY.

Trees you meen? he says.

Genrally, I says.

I ent bad I spose, he says. Why?

Cos one o us will need to, I says. Myte be better that tis me but I thawt best to ask.

At letters when we is shore none can overhear us, I tells him o my plan.

His eyes wyden.

Twill be a hard thing to pull off, he says and I nod.

I kno, I says, but we got to try.

When tho? he says. When do we do it?

First part we do this time next week. Beer Munday, I says. You be the distrakshun and Ill do the rest.

Shore? he says uncertain soundin. That ent no time at all to prepayre.

Shore, I says. We sets it up on Beer Munday and sets it off on followin Maykers Day. Tis the only way to do it. Else we wayte anuvver whole month for the chance again.

What if someone sees us eh? What if we get cawt?

Tis a risk we are goin to have to run, I says. But if all goes to plan, the Mayker will give all o Bearmouth a sine to remember for the rest o there lyves.

We are to do it then? he says and I nod.

Thomas told me, I says, his last words. He told me to get out o here. Twas his way o blessin what we are to do and for

185

that I am glad. Twas him in the dream that did give me the idea arfter all.

Devlin grins as the whissul goes for brayke.

We will go throo it all at letters tomorro, I says.

And when we do get to mess, tis straynge but I do find my appertyte beginnin to come back.

I hold Thomas in my thawts all mornin. The monthlees have long gone as he sed they wuld, ent nothin but piss comin out now and tis lyke they had never come. I dearly wish he were here to talk to bout all this and all the uvver things. So much I want to say to him, so much I want to ask him. Bout his sister, bout letters. And I realize there ent no more letters now. Not really. Tis just a word we use for meetin, tis all.

Tobe gone. Thomas gone.

And I must needs get out o Bearmouth fore I go the sayme way as them.

All week at letters, Devlin and I run throo the plan whisper whisperin lyke mice. Cos what we are to do is both heethenish and full o daynger but we must do it. We must.

ON MAYKERS DAY AT GRUEL, I DOS IT. I arsks Jack if we can join him on Beer Munday in the mess. His fayce is lyke a book too eesily read.

We shall, all o us, drink a toast to Thomas, I says. I kno us youngs dunt normally come but shore Devlin is old enuff and tis troo that I must needs be near old enuff now. So, I says, can we come?

Jack looks at Skillen who tryes not to larf and Nicholson nods his head.

Newts grown up enuff, he says. Thats for shore.

Will and Joe nod too as they eat the last o their shuggard gruel.

Jack sighs to hisself. Your days as a young is numberd Newt, he says. You wuld o corse be most welcome. Youre old enuff.

I pretend to pick up a tankard and rayse it to him. Jack near dos mayke me fall over wi his slap slappin me on the back in joy.

I ent shore I lykes the tayste o beer over much but tis somethin I must at leest show willin on. Devlin too. Our plan dos depend upon it.

I DUNT SING ON MAYKERS DAY BUT MOUTH THE WORDS WHILST INSTED I ABSORB ALL I CAN SEE AS BEST I CAN. How many steps before the entrance to the Hall. How far from wall to wall, how fast I can run, how high I must needs climb. How long it will all tayke. I am smaller and more nimball, just lyke the creetures that are my naymesake and so twill be me that climbs the Mayker we have agreed. I look up at the Maykers fayce and all I can think o is how long a fuse I will need as my maw opens and closes wi no sound comin out.

I feels bad for those we are to lie to but, I thinks to myself, as I mouth the prayer, it ent no worse than how they has alreddy been deceevd by the Master.

TIS TIME. Tis Beer Munday and today is the day we must put our plan into playce.

Tis alryte, I thinks to myself. We can do this. We can.

Arfter shifts, we heads to the layke and I spyes Devlin who smyles at me and nods. We must do this. We must. For Tobe, for Thomas, for all o us in Bearmouth.

Tis the usual crackall o fire in the air arfter work on a Beer Munday. The men are ryte reddy for their drink, chompin their lips, slappin each uvver on the back.

As the uvvers head to mess, I heads back to the dorm, cayreful to put the panel across the doorway so as none can see in. I lifts up Tobes mattress and cayrefullee pulls out two sticks o dynamyte. I feel them, cold and hevvy in my hand lyke canduls but not. I pushs em down into my boots and layces em back up. Tis only when I goes to leeve that I remembers the fuses.

Stewpid Newt, I says in my head. Tis only two things you got to remember and you fayre forgot one o em. I goes back to the mattriss and pulls out a coil o fuse. Tis long so I rolls up the arm o my shirt and curls it ryte round and round, tuckin it in at the end so tis sayfe from pryin eyes.

I am reddy, I thinks to myself as I heeves the panel back to the side.

In the mess hall, as we eats our meet and tatties, the men all cheers and stomps their feet when the huge barrels o beer are rolled in. They chants beer beer beer and slaps the mess taybles hard enuff to mayke em shayke.

Big pewter tankards are handed round so the men taykes a mug each. We arnt alloud to keep em tho, all must be returnd at the end o the nyte else all that eat there pay a fine. What they think we will do wi the mugs elsewyse, Mayker only knos.

Jack stops the man handin out the tankards and taykes two xtra—one for me and one for Devlin.

Tis a fact they are old enuff now, he says.

The man looks at us, judgin us.

On your head be it, he says fore shruggin and movin on.

I have drunk waterd beer before but not lyke this. This stuff is strong. No wonder it dos turn the mens heads to mush and mayke them sick the next day. Men drinks and sings and larfs, they stands on the taybles and sings lyke fools. I sips at my beer, ekin it out fore I needs a cleer head for what I am to do.

Devlin joins in some o the songs and I frowns at him. He looks lyke he is fayre enjoyin hisself too much and I worry that we carnt pull our plan off if he is not stone cold sober.

Jack clambers up onto the tayble and joins in a rousin song and Devlin is hauld up besides him. I smyles and cheers and claps but I want to kick him so Mayker help me. I carnt do this on my own.

Devlin knoks into Jack and spills a load o his beer on both me and the tayble and he larfs his head off before stumblin back down and onto me.

Cheer up Newt, he whispers in my ear. Got to look lyke I really am drunk.

I hiss at him, Well mayke shore you ent.

The evenin wears on and I carryes on pretendin to tayke sips o my beer. The rowdiness gets louder tho some men do alreddy look lyke they have had more than enuff and sit slumpd up on the walls snorin and hiccuppin to thereselves wi foul burps.

Devlin leans up gainst me, swayin slightly. I feels cross wi him. We will have to wayte anuvver whole month if we are to try again. A whole month waysted.

He leans up and whispers in my ear. Is it convincin enuff? he says.

I elbows him and he snorts wi a larf.

Leanin back into me, he whispers in my ear. Reddy? he says.

But he dunt wayte for a reply as he goes to stand and then harf falls over onto me.

Hes had too much, I says to Jack. Ill tayke him back.

I hoists Devlin up and lets him lean into me but I ent full shore if hes pretendin or if he actually is rollin drunk.

As we staggers out o the mess, leavin our tankards behind, we treads past the pair o guards who stand on watch.

Hes had too much, I mutters at them and they grins at us as we go past.

No sooner are we around the corner than I shoves Devlin off.

What you playin at? I says.

He grins at me and I sees from his eyes that he is near enuff sober as me.

Playin at bein sloshd, he says and mock punches me on the sholder.

Lets go, I says.

Arm in arm, I leads the way, listernin out quietly as we go. He knoks my leg at one poynte and we stop.

Cayreful, I says to him, hissin, mindful o the dynamyte tucked in my boots.

He nods.

As we goes up the emptee tunnels we come across uvver drunks, some slumpd on the walls, uvvers curld up in baskets. I ent never seen the lyke before. All this just for a drink that tastes vile anyways.

Tis a way o manidgin the men, I thinks to myself. Get em wantin somethin, get em to pay for it and restrict access to it so that when they gets it they wants more o it. Lyke all things down here. Tis about control.

The guards ignore us. Two on each level at the start and end o each ramp upwards. They chats amongst themselves as I hefts Devlin up.

Had too much eh? they says, chucklin to thereselves. Always the sayme on Beer Munday ent it?

But I notiss that they got tankards themselves. Playin ryte into our hands they are.

I crosses my fingers and hopes for luck. Im so in the habit o askin for the Maykers help that it dos seem straynge to not say it.

Mayker protekt me, I says in my head. Mayker sayve us from harm.

When we are out o syte o the guards, we walks normally, closely together just in cayse. The guards always have a candul see so we sees their lytes flickrin which gives us plenty o warnin afore we sees em and they sees us. And the drunkards that see us, well, I carnt think any o them will remember much about this eve by the time the morro comes.

Bearmouth becomes more chill as we travel upwards but we move as quickly as we can knowin that tis only this nyte in the whole month that we have the chance to put the first part o our plan into action. I think o all the people workin

workin away on each level. Evry floor filled wi men and boys slayvin their guts out for the Master.

Two more levels and we are nearly there, Devlin hiccuppin and burpin past the guards at the bottom.

I dunt kno your fayces, says one o the guards. Stop there.

I drag Devlin to one side, heart in my mouth, hammerin away.

Sorry Sir, I says, tis just that hes drunk and—

Ah, leeve em, says the uvver guard. Hes drunker than John Marshall got that time, look at the stayte o him. What harm are two drunk youngs goin to do eh? Mayke shore you get yourself back to your dorm. Work tomorro dunt forget.

No Sir, I says. Tis just that he wantd to see his bruvver from one o the higher levels and tis the only day he could do it bar Maykers Day.

No gatherin, says the first guard. You kno the rules.

Go on wi you, says the second guard. Dunt be such a miseree eh Quinn? Let em go. Go on.

Devlin raises a maginary tankard towards them both.

Cheers fellas, he says, I will drink to your health.

It ent until we are out o view that I allow myself to breeth again.

That was too close, I whispers.

As we reetch the ryte level and head towards the Maykers Hall, all is quiet and I feel Devlin skweeze my hand in the dark. Nearly there. Then a lyte flickers and I hears voyces echoin in the Maykers Hall.

Devlin pushs me to one side.

Tis our chance, he whispers. Go. I will distrakt them.

He staggers on ahead o me lookin as drunk as the men in the mess. He mutters to hisself, swayin to and fro.

Two guards come into view and I hides behind the rocks at the entrance o the Hall as Devlin swaggers towards em.

Ah frends, he cryes fore burstin into song.

They larfs out loud when they sees him and he heads towards em wi arms outstretched.

Fellas, join me in a song, he says burpin loudly at em.

You carnt be goin to the Maykers Hall, one o em says. Tis not alloud this eve.

Ah tis a shayme, says Devlin hiccuppin and swayin. Fore Id o lyked to thank him for inventin the most divine and delishuss drink o beer. Fellas, tis a shayme you ent got no beer here, you is missin out see.

They larfs and sing songs together as Devlin steers em down the tunnel away from the Maykers Hall and I sneeks in. A candul burns either side o the entrance but inside tis dark.

Mayker protekt me, I says as I go past the canduls and into the hall. I close my eyes and sydle in.

Feelin the damp hard rock under my hands, I edges ryte round the hall. I must needs be quick workin in the dark. I bends down and pats the sticks o dynamyte in my boots and then tippy tose quiet as a spyder fast as I can over to the Mayker hisself.

I shivers as I stand before him, feelin him lookin down at me and I tell myself over and over. He ent here. He ent here. I hold my hands tyte to my chest and think o Thomas. I must do this. I must. Not for me, not for Devlin but for all o us in Bearmouth. For Jack, for Skillen, for Nicholson, for the Davidsons. For evry single one o us.

I hears Devlin and the guards maykin jokes outside. My heart is fayre in my mouth as I skweeze past as far as I can round the Maykers side, as far to the back o him as I can and begin to climb up him, hands and feet fumblin as I go up. I ent climbd lyke this ever but I am strong from years o draggin and haulin hevvy baskets and I pulls myself up and up as fast as I can.

The voyces outside get louder and I fears they are a comin in but Devlin must steer em away somehow and the larfter echos throo the Hall afore faydin. I feel the Mayker under my hands as I climbs, feels it brush against my fayce and there ent no power there, no strength, tis just rock, sayme as the walls o Bearmouth, sayme as the walls o the dorm.

It taykes what feels lyke forever to get to the top but then I feels it, the top o the roof brushin gainst my head and I must be there—the Maykers head itself. Tis here that I must needs lay the dynamyte. I wedges the first stick in underneeth the neck o the Mayker testin it a fayre few times to mayke shore it dos stay tyte. Then anuvver the uvver side o the neck, wedgd tytely in too. The fuse must be long enuff to reetch near to the ground else all fails. I unweeves it from my arm where tis hidden under my shirt. I swallows wi nerves as I do it.

I clambers back down, harder than goin up as I carnt feel my footholds so eesily and a few times I near lose my footin and fear I will fall back into nothin. Tis only when I am sayfe back down and can feel my feet on the floor o the Hall that I lets myself breeth a little more easy. The fuse is only just about long enuff and I tucks it up and under, rollin it back up and then reetchin back up to hide it from view on a little nook as high as I can stretch up.

Tis dun.

Six more days and we will be back here, Devlin and I. Back in the Maykers Hall and the next part o our plan will be put into action. But for now, all I can hope is that all lays undiscoverd til then.

I sneeks back out o the Hall listernin to Devlin and the guards afore I dares come out o the entrance. Devlin whissuls to himself loudly and I kno tis the signal that all is well. I comes out o the shadows and pretends I just cayme up the tunnels.

Mayker protekt him, I groans as I goes over to Devlin and the guards. Shore I am sorry for my frend, tis the first time he dos have beer this eve. I been lookin for him all over. I do hope he ent been borin you to tears wi his drunk talkin, I says rollin my eyes.

The guards larf at me and pats me on the head and says what a nyce lad I am for lookin arfter my frend and they sends us both off sayin they do hope he dunt have too bad a headayke tomorro.

Tis dun, I whispers to Devlin when we are out o ear o the guards.

He sighs wi relief. You took so long I thawt we was to be discoverd, he says. Tis an effort to pretend to be that drunk for so long. All is well? he says and I nod.

The fuse is hidden down the back, it just needs one o us to reetch up and lyte it and then . . .

The sine, whispers Devlin.

The sine, I says back to him.

We heads back to dorm wi out further trubble. The guard who tryd to stop us ent on duty when we go back and all is well. For now at leest.

THE DAY ARFTER BEER MUNDAY EVRYONE IS FEELIN SOREHEADED SAYVE ME AND DEVLIN. Jack is impressd that Devlin seemd to drink so much beer and yet has no hangover.

Tis lyke I was as a lad, he says, slappin him on the back. Tis hard to drink so much beer now as the years do weigh hevvy upon me but this lad is good at holdin it.

We works hard all day but worry nags me. Did I hide the fuse well enuff? What if someone was to go round the back o the Mayker and see the fuse or even the sticks o dynamyte? What if what if? I tryes to clamp down my worryes but I knos some o the guards myte recognyse Devlin again and I worrys for both o us.

The darkness haunts me now. Thomas and Tobe around me. I feel them. I feel all o the soles o those who ent here no more. Worse still, sometimes I fear I feels Walsh too. But I kno he ent wi the Mayker now, even if he was real. Walsh is somewhere far darker, where he belongs. Lyke the Devil he was.

I tryd goin to caban wi the rest o dorm yesterday. They talks about beer, about wimmin and they dos share storyes too. Not lyke those that Thomas and me and Tobe mayde up. Crude storyes, funny ones. It passd the time but I sits there thinkin how they could better use their time. Work together gainst the Master, stand together, but Jack has the loudest voyce and he dos shout down those who try and say anythin about chaynge or how things could be better.

Tis what it is and tis how it is, he says and he dunt listern uvverwyse.

See what happend to Thomas, he says. For all his learnedness, it dunt stop the Mayker taykin you when he wants to. Tis how it is.

So today, we sits me and Devlin and says insted that we are at letters. We bides our time. We plans and plots. A sine is comin see. A sine from the Mayker. And both o us must play our parts as well as we can.

TIS WEDDENSDAY WHEN A MAN WE DUNT KNO APPEARS AT MESS FIRST THING. Mr Sharp bows to the man formal lyke when he comes in as if he is in awe o him. I think at first that he is there for us. That Devlin and I have been cawt, found out. But I am wrong. He ent here for us. He is here for somethin else.

Mr Sharp rattles a spoon on a bowl to get our attenshun.

Listern listern, he says loudly. He poyntes at the bord on the wall. The Master ent too pleased that this last week the produktivitee o Bearmouth is less than the week afore. It ent good enuff so unless this week is better, your wayges will be dockd.

A groan echos round the hall.

That ent all, says Mr Sharp. This ere is Mr Lewis and he has been poynted Inspektor o Bearmouth lyke. And he has somethin to say too.

I looks at Mr Lewis. He looks lyke a rat in green tweed. All little and wiry and nose and whiskers and wi a small pair o glasses perched on the end o his nose. Mr Lewis dos narrow his eyes at us.

Men, he says in a voyce that is calm but commandin. Men and boys o Bearmouth. I have worked in many o the Masters mines and this is the worst I have ever seen.

You an me both mayte, shouts a voyce and a chuckle goes around.

Mr Lewis waytes for calm and then steps forwud. Who sed that? he says and evryone looks at their boots. Who sed that? he says more firm lyke. And the room dos go so quiet you could hear a beetalls foot steps.

Mr Lewis stays where he is. Who. Sed. That. He says again, slow lyke.

A man stands up, nudgd up to standin.

Come here man, Mr Lewis says, beckonin him forwud. Come here. To the front, where all can see you.

The man dunt move at first.

Here, says Mr Lewis loudly and the man walks forwud, starin at his feet lyke he dos wish he was anywhere else but here. He stops in front o Mr Lewis.

You think what I say is funny? says Mr Lewis all teeth and snarl.

The man sniffs and stares at his feet. Mayker sayve us, says Jack under his breath.

You think what I say is funny? says Mr Lewis again, sayin each word lyke a sharp dagger. Starin at the man as he dos so.

No Sir, says the man findin his feet awfull interestin lyke. It ent funny at all.

No, says Mr Lewis. No it is not. Your wayges shall be dockd in harf for your insolents. Mr Sharp mayke note o his nayme. Harf wayges for three weeks. I think that is a fayre punnishment for insolents.

There is an intayke o breath around the hall. Harf pay for three weeks is harsh for a simple joke.

You may return to your seat, he says to the man who dos look in trooth lyke he has harf shrunk in hyte.

That is what happens when you do not obey your betters, says Mr Lewis. Akshuns have contseekwences. So in future, he says calm as anythin. In future. You will do xactly what I say. Understood?

There is a murmer o assent that goes round the hall. Yes Sir, yes Sir.

Now, says Mr Lewis. It has come to my attenshun that not only is this mine slack in terms o productivitee but also that there are men and lads too who have been labelld awkwud men in the past and may harbor some resentment towards the manidgment o Bearmouth. I say to you all. Stop. Put your past behind you. For I say now that any smell and any tayste I get o rebellion in this mine will be crushd underfoot. And wi that in mind, anyone who tells Mr Sharp in confeedents o someone who myte be a plottin or a plannin somethin and that man or boy is found giltee by my good self, the person who did tell will get a months salary for free and . . . he pauses lyke. And free beer for a month for their whole dorm.

A murmer and mutterin dos go round the hall. Dobbin on anuvver man is tell taylin and goes against the rules o work here. I wonders if Mr Lewis sees what I see, that men will mayke any ol nonsense up for a chance o a months salary for free. He will be crushd wi the wayte o all the tell taylers. But my moment o thinkin this soon dissolves lyke shuggar in water when I see the watchfulness o the eyes o the men glancin and dartin over evryone else. The waryness o all. The atmosphere in here has gone from the usual warmth o men and lads chattin to coldness lyke ice. This dunt bode well.

Evryone watchin their backs eh, growls Jack.

I shall be visitin each o you in turn at your playce o work to see how we can improve produkshun, says Mr Lewis. You will all be seein me in the next week. All I ask is that you answer my questions and you do your work to the best o your ability.

The silence hangs in the hall.

Good, says Mr Lewis. You may continue wi your gruel.

Devlin looks over at me. He holds one hand out on the tayble, flat, and stretches out three fingers. One for each day. Three more days o work arfter today and then tis Maykers Day. Three more days until our plan either sayves us or undos us.

TIS NOT TIL FRIDAY MORNIN WHEN WE SEES MR LEWIS AGAIN.

The first we knos o it is when we sees a bryte lyte comin down
the tunnels, a steddy lyte, not lyke our canduls. He is flankd
wi two guards who are both holdin sayfety lamps for him.

My heart tis fayre in my mouth thinkin that someone has
told tales on us but then I remember that Mr Lewis says he
was visitin each o us in turn.

He stops near me and Jack and so we stops our work.

No no, he says, wayvin his arm at us. Continue as if I am
not here.

One o the guards opens up a folded stool and Mr Lewis
sits down on it.

We tryes to work as hard as we can but tis odd havin
someone watch you and such bryte lytes in your eyes an all.

When the whissul goes for brayke, Mr Lewis comes
closer as we put our tools down. He has a small notepad and
a fountin pen that he dos use to write. One o the guards
holds out a pot o ink for him to dip it into as he maykes
notes.

Naymes? he says and we both answers, Jack first as hes
older and then me. Roles? Mr Lewis says.

Hagger and trayler, we says.

He poyntes at our basket. How many a day? he says.

Varies, Jack says but we runs throo the numbers o good
days and bad days and Mr Lewis writes em all down and
comes up wi an average.

Not pleasin, he says lookin disappoyntd wi us.

Jack coffs loudly and then descends into a proper coffin fit. Mr Lewis waytes impayshuntly til he dos stop. Jacks hankercheef is full o black spewtum and for the first time I sees bits o blood in it too. Drops o red.

Mr Lewis asks us more questions, how often our kwipment needs replaycin, what size mandrils we use, all sorts o things til we are fayre worn out wi talkin to him.

Tis only when he is dun that he folds his little notepad aways and puts it in his pockit, pattin it lyke a dog as he stands up, and one o the guards silently folds his chair back up.

Newt Coombes, he says. Newt. Yes, I remember that nayme, it has come up elsewhere. He looks at me wi his flint cold eyes lyke a snayke lookin at a mouse. I shall be watchin you closely chylde, he says. I shall watch all o you here in this mine lyke a hawk. He smyles at me for a moment fore turnin and headin off.

I dunt lykes that man, growls Jack.

I wayte and watch the lyte fayde away down the tunnels.

Me neether Jack, I says. I dunt lykes him and I dunt trusts him neether.

TIS SATURDAY AND THE DAY AFORE MAYKERS DAY. I am bidin
my time. I have gone throo it all so many times in my head,
in my dreams, as I work in the dark that it seems to me that
I have lit that fuse a hundred times or more.

But I kno I ent. And I kno all dos rest on tomorro.

If we get cawt, we will shore be hangd for it.

I whispers that to Devlin once and he shruggd.

Better hangd topside and one more glance o the sky than
be crushd down here in the coal, he says.

Praps hes ryte.

Trooth be told I am havin second thawts sometimes.
What happens when we get out? I thinks about Ma and
I dunt rytely knos quite where the farm is. I ent got a
proper nayme and I ent got a proper home. Far away is
what Thomas sed, go far away from here. But then I thinks
about what Ill do to earn a crust and all that and I feel
fayre panickd about it all. Then I see Jacks blood spatterd
handkee and I think we got to get out. Tis what Thomas sed.
We got to get out. Come what may.

Tis how my thawts go all day, one way and then tuvver all
the time, to and fro to and fro lyke me goin up and down
the rolley roads wi the coal. To and fro to and fro.

At mess in the eve, theres a buzz, Maykers Day tomorro,
a day o rest and all are glad o a brayke. I am so worn out that
I dos near fall asleep into the meets and tatties but Devlin
nudges me and I manidges to stay awayke. Tobe once fell
asleep strayte into his plate. We did fayre larf at him wi his

fayce all coverd in grayvee and meets. Now tho I thinks back on it and I ent findin it funny no more.

Tis our last eve afore the plan. I feel strayngely calm as I looks around the mess at the tired fayces and think how, if all goes well, we will all be free by this time tomorro.

Free.

And I will breeth the fresh air o outside once again. Even if I dunt rytely kno where Ill be headin arfterwuds.

I DURNT SLEEP CAYSE I WAYKES UP LATE. So I lies there on my back, starin into nothinness, rackd wi muddld thawts.

I think o Thomas and Tobe. O Walsh too.

I think o before I cayme here. O those glimpses o life before.

I think o all the years o singin to the Mayker. All those prayers.

I think o all the bred and meet eaten over the years. O swimmin in the layke. O the little white fishes nibblin my tose. O how Thomas kept me sayfe.

I think o bein older. O bein a wimmin.

I think o Devlin too. O how I thawt he was the Devil in disguys and how he has insted become a troo frend.

I think o all these things til the thawts becomes so hevvy that they weighs down my brayne and I drifts off into fitful sleep full o dreams I dunt remember. I waykes up wi damp sheets coverd in sweat.

All else is asleep. I hears em snufflin and snorin around me and I realize this is my last nyte here. If all goes to plan, this is my last nyte here in this playce. I think o the lynes I drew on the wall to mark Tobe comin back too.

I dunt sleep anuvver wink til evryone else starts stirrin and the day begins anew.

Mayker sayve us, I says to myself under my breath as I throw back my blanket. I scratchs out the lynes on the wall wi my nyfe. May all go well today, I says to myself.

I look at Devlin and I see he is as pale as me. I bet he ent slept a wink neether.

Maykers Day, bellows Jack. Sayve and protekt us Mayker, he says.

Amen, I says loudly.

Amen, says Devlin catchin my eye.

And so it begins.

I FEELS SICK TO MY STOMARCK AS WE WENDS OUR WAY UP TO THE MAYKERS HALL. I durnt eat a thing at gruel. Not even the sweetniss o the shuggar can brayke throo my nerves.

I holds my hands out in front o me and they dos wobball from side to side.

Tis the shaykes is all, whispers Devlin. Twill be alryte.

I nods.

I feels sick and all, he says and I nods.

We will be alryte, I says back to him. I feels in my pockit to mayke shore my match tin is there. I dunt tell Devlin neether but I keeps the spayre stick o dynamyte in my boot too. Just in cayse.

Tis all or nothin today.

I crosses my fingers behind my back. Jack always told me not to do that when I was little, sed it was fayre superstishun and the Mayker dunt approve o the old ways but I dunt cayre. I needs all the help I can muster.

We walks into the Maykers Hall, all the canduls flick flickrin and Devlin is ryte by my side.

I feels him skweeze my hand. Tis our signal.

As evryone files in, orderly lyke, from all over Bearmouth, I taykes my chance and slips away in the crowd, gentlee pushin myself over to the uvver side o the Hall where dozens o men are alreddy jostlin up gainst each uvver for spayce and to get the best view o the Mayker. Wi all the movement the canduls flick flicker and shadows loom and disappeers all over the Hall. My heart flit flutters in my chest lyke a bird as I slips over to the far end near the front.

The Mayker is there in front o me. Standin tall over us. I looks cayrefullee lyke but there ent no sine o anythin amiss. Either I hid it all as well as I hoped or someone has discoverd us.

I tryes to swallow but there ent no spit in my mouth and I wonders for a moment if I sweatd all the moisture off in the nyte. I slowly maykes my way to the front but I feels a hand on my sholder stoppin me.

Tis a man I dunt kno but he is smylin at me.

Dunt do to get too close to the Mayker eh, he says.

He smyles but his grip is firm. I am at the front o the far edge o the crowd all buzzin and hummin wi energy and yet calm and quiet. The Mayker is ryte in front o me, bare spittin distance away, the wall o the Hall hemmin me in to the ryte. So close but not close enuff.

I carnt do it. I carnt get to the fuse. I carnt get away wi this man watchin me, wi his hand holdin me back.

I look around in desperayshun for Devlin but I carnt see him neether. I am at the front o a sea o strayngers. Adrift.

I want to cry but tears come there none.

Tis only a week, I says to myself. One more week and we can try again. Praps this man ent gonna be here in this sayme playce next Maykers Day. Tis just bad luck is all.

Suddenlee the Hall goes quiet. Mr Sharp comes in to lead the prayers as he always dos but this time two uvvers are wi him. I straynes to see as all else do lean forwud blockin my view, but then I sees him. Tis the Master himself, his hat tall on his head as ever, followd by Mr Lewis.

My heart beats twyce as fast. Tis him. The Master. He

must kno o our plans. My head is all a whirlin as the Master and Mr Sharp come to the front.

The Master ent ever here on Maykers Day. I ent ever seen him before in the Hall.

A murmer goes ryte round the Hall as evryone pushs further forwud to get a better look. I hears the whispers around me, some alreddy sayin tis the Master.

Settle down settle down, says Mr Sharp holdin his hand up to indicayte for quiet.

The rumblins turn into a hushed awe. I edges forwud and sees Devlin at the front o the crowd almost ryte in front o the Master. I catches his eye and he looks frytend, lyke he did when he first cayme here. A newborn foal.

Mr Lewis you kno alreddy, says Mr Sharp. And this, he says, waytin for the whisperin to quieten. This is Mr Johnson. The Master hisself.

There is a gasp from the crowd. The mythikal beest here in front o them. And I wonders if any o them see what I see. He may be many things, the owner o the mine, a bully, but he is also just a man. Flesh and blood lyke the rest o us.

He is here today to offer a speshul prayer, says Mr Sharp. On akkount o the fact that we needs to up the produktivitee o the mine.

The Master steps forwud and I see it. The moment he sees Devlin. I see his fayce, puzzld at first, tryin to playce him and then the realisayshun o who he is.

I see Devlin step forwud too, a moment between them and then Devlin holds his head up, lookin up to the roof.

He is here, Devlin yells in a straynge voyce. The Mayker, he is here. I can feel him!

He jerks his body lyke he is havin a fit. To and fro he

dances. The Mayker is inside me, he sings. He is inside all o us.

What on earf is the lad doin? I thinks to myself. Tis lyke he is havin a fit.

Mr Sharp steps forwud but so dos Jack who holds up his hand.

Tis a sine, says Jack. Then again, louder, turnin to the whole hall. Tis a sine, he yells. The Mayker has blessd this lad.

The Mayker, cryes Devlin. The Mayker! He is here!

The man behind me pushs me out o the way as the crowd surges further forwud to get a better look. Whilst all are lookin at Devlin, at this boy shaykin wi the glory o the Mayker, I taykes my chance and wriggalls out o the crowd. I whispers thanks to Devlin for his quick thinkin as I dashs forwud, not twentee foot or more, and round the edge to the back o the Mayker. I waytes a moment, heart thump thumpin in the shadows, and yet nobody drags me back out.

Theres anuvver one, I hear someone cry and I hear someone else shoutin too. The Mayker. He is here. Tis a diffrent voyce tho, one I ent recognisin. Tis lyke a fever creepin over the Hall.

Look here, says the Master loudly.

The Mayker, the Mayker, chants Devlin, drownin him out, uvvers joynin him now, their voyces comin together. The Mayker is here. The Mayker.

I carnt see anythin from behind the rocks but I must needs do what I cayme here to do and I thanks Devlin a thowsand times for causin a distrakshun. I reetches up but there is nothin. Bare rock is all.

I stretch and reetch and pray and sob.

Come on, come on, I whispers. Come on.

And then. At the tip o my fingers. The fuse.

I works it free wi my fingers til the end drops down.

The feverd chantin gets louder and louder as I pulls out my tin o matchiss. I hold it in my hand and wayte a moment. All stands before me. Is this really our only way out? I looks at the fuse in my hand and the tin in the uvver.

Mayker sayve me, I whispers. Mayker sayve us all.

I strykes a match and lytes the fuse. The chantin hides the fizzin sound as the spark weeves its way up up and towards the head.

Tis dun. And it cannot now be undun.

SILENCE! SHOUTS MR SHARP AS I SNEEKS A LOOK FROM BEHIND THE ROCK THAT I USED TO THINK WAS ALL THINGS TO ALL PEOPLE. The Mayker mayde meerly o stone sted o godliness.

Devlin is jerkin and singin and those around him are singin too, there are uvvers shaykin an all, a handful o mainly young lads but Devlin ent alone.

Mr Sharp goes towards him and slaps Devlin round the fayce.

Stop it, he says loudly. He taykes him by the sholders. Stop it, he says again and shaykes him. Stop it, stop it!

Jack steps forwud. Leeve the boy alone, he says. The Mayker dos talk throo him see.

Uvvers crowd behind Jack, backing him up. Mr Sharp releeses Devlin, too startld to speke no more.

The Master watches all this and taykes a step backwuds. It feels lyke the whole room could ignite wi power. For some reason he turns, and at that moment he sees me. I feel him, his eyes borin down on me.

But tis too late. I hears a rumble and I runs out and back into the crowd.

That boy, shouts the Master as he dos poynte to me. That boy there.

The Mayker spekes! cryes Devlin drownin him out. The Mayker spekes!

Devlin poyntes to the Maykers head and, as he dos so,

the dynamyte goes off. It dos look lyke fire comin out o his head and Devlin screetches.

Tis a sine, he yells. The Mayker is here!

Evryone else starts chantin now, the Mayker, the Mayker!

Tis a sine, Devlin shouts and I shout it too from harfway in the crowd.

Tis a sine! Tis the sine! Tis the sine the Mayker promisd us!

A straynge man next to me grabs me and holds me by the sholders.

Is it the sine chylde? Is it? he says eyes glintin.

Tis shorely a sine, I say, tis <u>the</u> sine is it not?

And then I looks beyond him and gasp.

The Maykers head is loose at the neck and as I look it dos roll forwud, perchd for one moment on the sholders afore tumblin down.

I screems and scrambles backwuds as the whole crowd in the hall lurches back. Hundreds o men lurchin and stumblin. The giant rock bounces down missin me by inches and shatterin into huge peeces.

Tis a sine! I shout. Tis a sine. Lyke the Maykers Prayer tells us, we are free, we are free!

I look at Devlin and he dos a tiny nod at me fore shoutin, We are free! The Maykers sine. We are free.

Jack joins in, his growly voyce rumblin. The Maykers sine is here! We are free men, free lads all. He wypes tears from his eyes. We are blessd all o us, the Mayker frees us today! The sine is here!

The crowd starts to cheer, chantin chantin, the sine the sine! We are free! We are free! The shout goes up. We are free!

The guards are joynin in too. They dashs out the

doorway joynin uvver men and lads elbowin and shovin
and crowdin to get out o the Hall, pushin and jostlin to get
out o there, up towards the next levels and up up to the lift
sharft.

I carnt quite believe my own eyes.

No, yells the Master. No! This is not the sine!

But his voyce is drownd out by the sheer wayte o men
shoutin. He clutches hopelesslee at those fylin past him at a
rate o nots, arms flaylin as he dos. He grabs at em, tryin to
stop em. No, this is not the sine! No! Stop! No! This is not
the sine!

We are free, we are free, yell the men. The sine, the
sine, the Mayker has freed us!

They shouts and cheers as they skweezes out o the hall in
a hurrikayne o kayoss and noyse.

More and more men heads out pushin and shovin throo
the narrow doorway as Mr Sharp and Mr Lewis tryes to hold
em back.

No, they say, no!

But ent none listernin to em now.

I looks behind me at whats left o the Maykers head where
it lies in the Hall, gentlee pitchin from side to side and, as
I looks at it, I dos wonder how I did ever think twas anythin
uvver than a pile o rocks.

Devlin elbows his way back throo the crowd towards me,
men partin reluktantly as he forces his way throo.

Newt, he says. We did it, he says, shaykin and pale as
people flow around us and out. We bloody did it.

I look for the uvvers but they are gone alreddy. The Hall
empteein lyke water out o a broken buckit as men fyle their
way out.

Jack and the dorm were some o the first out, says Devlin

and he hugs me. We did it Newt, he says in my ear, above the sounds o the noyse in the Hall. We did it.

I glances to the ryte o the entrance and the Master is flat against the wall watchin Mr Sharp and Mr Lewis tryin to stop the flood o men afore them. But then Mr Sharp disappeers in the crush, his head bob bobbin out amongst a sea o men and tis just Mr Lewis left grabbin at men tryin to stop the flow but he can no more stop em than a rat stop a herd o bulls.

Come on, Devlin says, lettin go o me. Come on. We got to go too.

But I carnt help but stop a moment and tayke it in. Men pushin and pullin at the doorway, forcin their way out, elbowin uvvers out the way to get out and up to the sharfts.

We have destroyd it, I thinks to myself, harf deaf wi the chants and screems and shouts as the Hall dos start to emptee around us, men jostlin me and Devlin out o the way and pushin past as they head out. I stands still and lets all that I have dun sink in. We have dun it. We have freed Bearmouth.

I see Mr Lewis carryd away in the throng too, arms wayvin as hes forced out the hall, swept up in the crowd. I see horror cross the Masters fayce. Tis just him left out o the manidgers now.

But then there is anuvver rumble and a rock falls on me, grayzin the top o my sholder and rippin my shirt. A handful o rocks crumble down around us and the air starts fillin wi dust, blowin out some o the canduls.

Come on, shouts Devlin, as the Hall darkens around us and men and lads push around us lyke a current in the layke, pullin and shovin us. We got to get out o here, it ent sayfe no more!

And then there he is. In front o us, the Master standin as still as he can as the crowd pushs past him. He steps towards us steddily and determind, elbowin uvvers out o the way as he dos so. His hat dusty and his suit torn, the polish o him long gone. And altho there are dozens and dozens o men pushin their way out around us it feels lyke we is the only three people in the whole world.

You, he shouts, poyntin at me. And you. I myte o known. I should o got rid o you when I had the chance, he snarls at Devlin. Just lyke your farver, the Master says as he pushs his way towards us. A rotten apple scared o the realitees o life. Lyke farver lyke son.

Theres a nasty look on his fayce and he dos pull somethin out o his pockit but then someone pushs him from the side and he dos trip backwuds into the crowd.

He yells, No, no!

But tis too late. He disappeers into the throng, hat bobbin til it falls off and out o syte as the mass o men lurches and surges out the doorway.

The crush pushs us forwud too and I carnt breeth.

Devlin, I whispers, Devlin!

He grabs my arm.

Help, I says in my head, my voyce crushd to nothinness. Help me.

The Hall rumbles behind us and Devlin glances back. He pulls me to the side, shovin his way out and clutchin my arm, draggin me wi him and we slowly edge sideways out o the push o the crowd.

I cling to the edge o the Hall gettin my breath back as men fyle out around us but then I hears a crackin noyse lyke when wood dos begin to split but o so much louder. I looks back up at the Mayker and cracks do appear in his body,

spreadin lyke likwid cross his torso and towards the arms.
The whole Hall rumbles around us, ground shudderin
under our feet. Theres a terrifyin splittin noyse as the
Mayker braykes in two and the top harf o his body toppalls
over, hittin the ground wi a loud thud. The rumbles echo in
myne ears and the floor shaykes violently.

The Hall emptees around us as the dust rises in clouds.
The last men and boys leeve the Hall and heads out towards
the lift sharfts. Towards the uvver side.

Alryte? says Devlin and I nod.

Look at what we have dun, I says.

He skweezes my sholder.

Come, he says. Tis time for us to tayke our leeve too.

I looks back at the Mayker above the risin cloud o dust
and see more cracks formin and wydenin. Devlin pulls me
forwud and we joins the last remnants o the men shufflin
out, bottle nekkd by the tunnels leadin up and out to the
sharfts. Chantin, shoutin. The hall rumbles and crumbles
behind us as the dust snuffs out more o the canduls.

I gasps as I step into the dark passidgeway, harf a dozen
bodies o men crushd underfoot lyin where they fell as the
last men in the mine shuffall and tramps forwud ahead o us.

And then I sees it. His hat, the Masters hat, skwashd flat.
I goes to pick it up and see that he is there too. Trampld on
and slumpd up gainst the uvver side o the wall, one leg at
a straynge angle. His fayce white as the blind fishes in the
layke. The dust hangs in the tunnel lyke mist.

I feel Devlin grip my arm as the Master turns his fayce
to us. We taykes a step back and I feels the ground shift
under us.

You can destroy Bearmouth, he says, breethin fast, but
so help me I will tayke you down wi it too, he says wi a leer.

There is somethin in his hand, small and shiny. He aims it towards us and I feels somethin whizz past my fayce burnin hot gainst my cheek.

I nearly lose my footin and then a bang sounds. The Master aims the thing towards the roof. A rock falls, a small one at first then some more, larger rocks. I steps forwud but Devlin pulls me back. The Master goes to say somethin else but the rocks loosen and fall on him as the roof cayves in.

Tis me who dos pull Devlin back this time, both o us scramblin backwuds. I trip and falls and I see all that follows.

No! No! the Master cryes as he holds his arms up. No!

But we never hear no more fore tis lyke an avalanche fallin on him, rocks steddy as rain, crushin the Master to dust.

I find myself screemin.

Devlin drags me back and we stands there huddld gainst the sides o the tunnel as the lyte o the last canduls on the passidgeway are blockd out bit by bit as the rocks fall and fall and fall and then we carnt see nothin no more.

All is blackness.

Hope faydes in me lyke a candul snuffd out.

I HOLDS THE WALL TO STEDDY MYSELF. Feel the rocks warm and wet under my hands.

The only way out. Blockd in front o us.

The Master crushd. Bearmouth empteed. We did what needed to be dun but now it seems we are to be punnishd for it.

Alryte? says Devlin in the dark.

He ent goin to hurt no one no more, I thinks, heart thumpin in my mouth, bile risin in my throte.

I dunt say nothin.

Newt, he says.

Im here, I says.

Where now?

Ent nowhere, I says. Tis the only way out.

We stays there in silence. Lettin it sink in.

Lyte a candul, he says. See how bad it is. We can dig our way out. We are strong ent we?

The mine rumbles again. I holds onto a post to steddy myself but I can feel that wobblin too.

Evrythins fallin apart, I says. The whole o Bearmouth comin apart at the seams lyke an old shirt.

Lyte a candul, he says, else I will.

Theres a spark o lyte and then Devlin is in front o me. The floor is wet, I see it now. Water that I am shore was not there before.

Devlin holds the lyte up by the rocks but most o em are

the size o a grown man. Tis playne to see that they are too hevvy for the lykes o the two o us to lift.

We are dun for, I says.

There must be anuvver way out, says Devlin, xaminin the rockfall. There must be.

I close my eyes and think—I thinks o Thomas and how I have faild him. I sayved the uvvers tis true, all those men and boys, most the whole o the workforce even now carryin their selves up the lift sharft sayve the handful in the passidgeway.

Not all got out then, I thinks. Not all.

Me and Devlin. Doomd to die here. In the warm blackness o Bearmouth. Joynin the Master in his dark grayve.

Mayker preserve us, I says to myself. Mayker sayve us.

I feels the walls rumble behind me again. The floor shayke shaykin.

We will be crushd to death, I says. The Mayker in the Hall, it must o been a weak spot for the mine. Twill come tumblin down around us.

There is always hope, Devlin says, still lookin at the rocks. Ent that what Thomas wuld say?

But Thomas ent here, I says.

I slides down the wall, feelin my back ruff gainst the post, the water splish splashin around my ankulls. I curls up and puts my arms tyte round my boots and tis then that I feels it.

The dynamyte. The spayre stick, round and hard lyke a candul.

I gasp.

What? says Devlin.

I reetches into my boot, pulls out the stick and shows him.

But then what use is it really? I says turnin it over in my
hand. We could blast the rocks here but tis just as lyke twill
set off anuvver rockfall and mayke things worse.

Tis worth a try, he says.

And then a thawt strykes me. I holds my hand up.

No, I says. No. I got a better idea.

What? he says.

Wild garlick, I says. Ent that what you calld it that time?
The flower you did draw.

Go on, he says.

See if we blasts our way throo here, even if there ent no
rockfall on our heads, tis as lyke that there myte be anuvver
collapse further up. We wuld as lyke still be stuck, I says. But
the wild garlick must needs grow above ground. Tis what
you sed. So we must be closer to gettin out there, see.

He grins at me, gettin ahead o himself.

So we blasts our way out o there, he says. Ha Newt! See,
there is always hope.

The walls shayke around us again as he helps me up to
my feet.

We must hurry, I says. We must hurry and find that drawin.

You kno the way? he says as we turn our backs on the
rockfall and heads down deeper into Bearmouth, our one
candul flickrin as we goes. Newt, Devlin says as we turns the
corner, you kno the way?

I nods, hopin beyond hope that Thomas will show me.

As we goes fast along the emptee rolley roads, I closes
my eyes evry now and then, just for a moment, as our feet
splish splash throo the dark water and I thinks o Thomas,
picturin him in my head. Rememberin him. Thinkin back
to all those times he did tayke me to the ponys and prayin
I dos remember the way.

Help me Thomas, I says to myself in my head. Help me.

There are piles o rocks in playces and some o the wooden supports across the roofs are broken, harf fallen in. We skweeze past em and neether o us says nothin but we both kno this is a one way trip.

Ent just the end o the Mayker this time, tis the end o Bearmouth and all.

Either we gets out o here forever or we lies here forever til we all do turn to dust.

WE SPLASHES PAST THE TUNNEL THAT LEADS TO THE DORM, PAST THE MESS HALL PASSIDGE AND IT DOS GET MORE NOISY WI THE RUN RUNNIN O WATER DOWN THE SIDES O THE WALLS AND STRAYNGE RUMBLES IN THE EARF ITSELF.

Down down we go, to the belly o the pit. Further further into deepest Bearmouth.

Tis down here, I says.

Devlin holds his candul up and looks, checkin down each post as I do the sayme on the uvver side.

There ent no flower.

Shore tis here? he says and in truth I ent.

I tryes to remember but all I kno is that tis on the way to the ponys and it ent a trip I did too often and so it ent a roote I kno well. Thomas always led the way see, sayve that las time we did go and see Boy. One tunnel is much lyke anuvver when you ent famileear wi em.

Tis further on, I says hopin beyond hope that I am ryte. Ent far, I says, just round the corner and down.

We go to carry on but Devlin stops me and his fayce dos go more pale than usual as we heads downwuds.

What? I says.

He looks down at the floor.

The water. Tis splish sploshin and harfway up my boots now. Worst o all, I can sees it risin.

We must hurry, I says and we carryes on til we come to a junkshun.

Left or ryte? says Devlin. Newt. Left or ryte?

I stand there and I dunt rytely kno.

Newt, he says. Please.

I holds out my hands hopin for a sine but there ent one.
I must guess tis all.

This way, I says and strides forwud to the left. I touch
the wooden post as I go throo for luck. Please let me be ryte,
I whispers to myself.

If the water carryes on gettin higher we ent even goin to
be able to see the flower, he says.

I nods, splashin throo the water as we xamine each post
in turn but all I sees is damp wood.

Devlin shouts. Here, he says. Newt! I found it. He hugs
me, nearly blowin out the candul. Tis here, he says.

I looks at it and I ent shore to be honest, I carnt truly
remember what he drew afore cept that twas a flower
I dunt kno.

Tis what I drew, he says. Am certain o it.

I looks at him in the flickrin lyte and I crosses my fingers.

Do it, he says. Lyte the dynamyte. Do it Newt.

Ent that simple, I says, sposed to drill a hole and—

We dunt have time for any o that, he says.

We could bring the whole playce down on our head,
I says.

I looks at him in front o me, the water swell swellin up
my calves, sinkin into my boots, throo the holes and into my
socks. Cold and wet. We stares at each uvver a moment.

Come on, I says. There must be a gap. However small,
must be, else you wunt o smelld it.

I peers and peers and tis too dark for a body to mayke
out anythin else but the ruggedness o the rocks.

Devlin holds the candul up close but I carnt see
anything. The water is rise risin all the time.

Got to mayke a decishun, I says, heart hammerin in my chest, feelin my panick risin wi the waters.

Do it, he says. Do it Newt. However you can. Tis our only chance.

I finds a smallish crevise smaller than my fist but big enuff to just hold the end o the stick o dynamyte.

Need small rocks to wedge it in, I says.

I feels the water wet on my nees and can feel the power o it rush rushin past me.

Ent got time for that, says Devlin and he pulls out a hankercheef and hands it to me. Ram it in wi that, he says.

Fuse ent long, I say.

Then we lyte it and run, he says.

Shore? I says.

He nods.

The stick holds steddy in the wall but tis a short fuse and it ent goin to give us more than a handful o moments to find shelter fore it blows.

Reddy? I says and he nods.

Go on, he says.

I fumbles in my pockit for my matchiss but as I go to lyte one my fingers are tremblin so much that I drops the whole tin.

It disappeers in the waters, lost.

I curse and curse but Devlin reetches into his pockit and offers me his tin.

Cayreful, he says and I nods.

Fingers tremblin I do it. I lyte the fuse.

Mayker sayve us, I says as he grabs the tin back.

And we run.

227

I AM UNDERWATER.

Bubbles shoot from my nose.

I am thrown lyke a rag doll in a river.

I scrabbles, arms weel weelin tryin to pull myself up to breeth.

I smack against the rocks.

Legs bashd. Arms bruisd.

I hit my head.

Pain.

Sharp sharp pain.

And then blackness.

AIR.

I choke.

Coff.

Air.

I breeth.

Gaspin. Raspin for more.

My head feels lyke I been batterd in all the fytes I did ever see.

Limbs lyke lead.

I groan.

I am alive.

Shallow water by my hands. I touch it.

Head back. Legs low.

I am bent over backwuds. Sore. Harf broken.

I remembers. The fuse. Runnin.

I am me.

I am alive.

And then I remembers.

Devlin. I whispers it.

Devlin.

I shouts it. Devlin. Shouts it again and again. Devlin. Devlin.

But answer comes there none.

SLOWLY I PULLS MYSELF UP TO SITTIN. Groanin achin all over.

I pull my legs to me and sit there in the dark. Wet all over, my clothin dos cling to me lyke a second skin. I feels the heat on my cheek where that thing the Master poynted did burn me. It feels sore lyke when my nostril was first slit in the mine. I listern but there ent nothin, just darkness.

Wherere I was swept to, this ent no outside. Tis as black as Bearmouth for shore. But I hear as I shouts Devlins nayme that this is some kind o cavern, my voyce dos ring back at me echoin round the walls.

This ent Bearmouth no more. This ent no mine. Tis a cayve that ent o mans maykin.

But it dunt matter much as seems to me I am no better off than before.

Trappd in the dark and no more dynamyte. I feels in my pockits and there are two stumps o canduls but then I remembers the matchiss. The droppd tin swept away. Devlins tin back in his hand.

I got lytes but nothin to lyte em wi.

And where so ever I am I dunt kno it. I carnt feels my way around.

I am all alone.

I hugs my legs tyte to me. Mind raycin away. No food. Even if I can drink the water, I ent goin to last long here.

Starvin away on my own in the dark.

I lets out a sob and it echos around. My own wailin comin back at me.

I sits there sob sobbin away til I am all out o tears.

Ent no good feelin sorry for yourself, I says to myself.

I dunt kno rytely how long I sits there for. Thinkin. Wondrin what to do. Starin into the blackness for what feels lyke forever.

Cos all o a sudden, there in the far distance. A tiny lyte flick flickers and wi it, a tiny bit o hope lytes in me. I ent alone arfter all.

I SHOUTS, DEVLIN DEVLIN, AND I HEARS IT ECHO ROUND ME.
Devlin Devlin.

And then o blessd relief.

Newt, I hears. Newt is that you? Newt Newt.

My own nayme dos wrap around me lyke a blanket.

I am alive.

And so is he.

I scrambles over rocks towards the lyte, splashin throo pools o water and stumblin towards him.

His fayce is bruisd and cut lyke Im shore myne is too.

You mayde it, he says and bursts into tears.

I hugs him so tyte that I fayre think Ill skweeze the very air out o him.

I am not alone.

I THAWT I WAS DUN FOR, I SAYS, MY OWN FAYCE WET WI TEARS AND STINGIN THE BURN ON MY CHEEK.

He nods, wypin his fayce.

Ent manly to cry, he says, sniffin.

I shrugs.

Dunt matter, I says. Dunt cayre bout any o that. We are alive. Both o us.

I thawt youd drownd, he says. Thawt I had too. Then cayme to here. Where are we?

I looks around me, candul flickrin as the wet wick struggles to stay alyte.

Tis a huge cavern the lykes o which I ent ever seen before. Bigger than the Maykers Hall. Bigger than anythin.

Look, he says.

On the far side theres what looks lyke a body leanin up against the cayve wall.

We goes over to it warily, the pair o us and Devlin holds the lyte up.

I recognize the fayce but he is o so much thinner now than when I saw him. Pale bruisd skin hangin off sharp cheeks.

Not banishd afer all then, I says. Tis Rickerbee. They must o left him to starve poor bugger. Somehow he got his way out o Bearmouth and mayde it out here.

I tayke Rickerbees cold hand, nobbly wi the drippins o his last candul, and skweeze it.

Tis alryte now fella, I says, none o em can do you no

233

more harm now. Not Walsh, not the Master, not none o
them. All gone forever and ever amen.

I smyles at Rickerbee and pats his hand and then I see
there is a faynte smyle on his fayce and he is lookin up and
so I look up too.

On the rocks above our heads there are animals drawn
in browns and reds and blacks. Herds o cattal or somethin
run runnin.

Pictures, I whisper. Look.

Devlin hands me the candul and I holds it up high gainst
the rocks. The lyte flickers and the animals do fayre look
lyke they myte run off the rocks and into real life.

I shivers.

Lyke magickal things, I say and then I sees it behind
Devlin. Red handprints on the wall. Three o them, diffrent
sizes. I holds my own hand up and playce it on top o the
middle one and it dos fit perfektly.

How long they been here for? I whispers.

Fore us, says Devlin. Fore Rickerbee. Fore time itself
praps.

Meens people been here before, I says. Meens theres a
way out.

Devlin snorts.

Thawt that before. And yet we still ent out are we? Still
in the dark. And Rickerbee never found a way out, that
much tis cleer.

How many canduls you got? I says and Devlin pulls out
one barely touchd candul.

I just got stumps, I says and holds mine out. No food but
we got your candul lit now, your spayre one, my stumps and
your matchiss too, I says. I dips my finger in the water by my
boots and taystes it. It dos seem alryte. Water and all, I says.

234

We got more than Rickerbee had, his last candul did melt all the way down til it was just drops in his hand. We got lytes tho, for a while at leest.

So, says Devlin. Which way now?

I poyntes strayte ahead where the cavern narrows down one end and it dos look awfull dark. Tis the direkshun the herds in the pictures do seem to be runnin in.

Shore? he says.

And I shrugs. Worth a try, I says.

He offers his hand and I taykes it.

Come on, he says.

Farewell Rickerbee, I says. Rest in peace.

Amen, says Devlin.

And the two o us head off into the darkness.

AT THE END O THE CAVERN IS A SMALL CREVISE, TYTE ENUFF THAT I CAN ONLY JUST SKWEEZE THROO IT.

I goes first, holdin Devlins candul til it is fayre too hard to hold it and push myself throo but I knoks it against the rock and pft it goes out. Darkness again.

You alryte Newt? I hears Devlin say from behind me.

Alryte, I shout back as best I can. Tis tyte around me as I pull and push myself throo. Twill be more o a skweeze for Devlin.

I scraypes my elbows throo and breethes out maykin my chest small and tyte, I tryes not to think about if I get stuck.

In the darkness, I remembers flashes o all that has happend. Thomas. Tobe. Walshs hands on me. The Masters fayce as the rocks tumbld towards him.

I closes my eyes and thinks o Thomas.

Please, I thinks. Please. One more push.

And then I am out. There is spayce, my arms are free. I pulls myself out and gingerly feel the walls around me, spayce enuff to stand but I hits my head on somethin and curse.

Newt, I hears him say. Newt.

Im alryte, I says. Tis tyte but Ill pull you throo.

It dos tayke an ayge to wriggall him out.

He cayrefullee lytes his candul when hes sayfely throo.

Fyve more matchiss left, he says, countin, but then our breath is fayre tayken away.

236

We stand in a faery ice land. White pillars reetch down from the roof and stretch up from the floor.

Tis what I must o hit my head on.

They gleam and glimmer in the lyte lyke pillars in a castle.

I reetch out and go to touch one and Devlin stops me.

What are they? he says. Are they sayfe?

Thomas once told me o such things, I says wi wonder in my voyce. Tis drippins from the rocks, salts and stuff. They must be hundreds o years old, I says as I gentlee touch one. Cold and wet under my hand. Lyke ice but not.

Tis wondrous, Devlin whispers and I smyles at him.

If I never live anuvver day Im glad I saw this one, he says.

I hold the candul up and the pillars go on and on into the distance.

Tis lyke nothin else, I say.

We move slowly throo the cayve o pillars, weevin our way, steppin over small ones, duckin our heads from the ones reetchin down.

I thinks o how Thomas wuld o loved to see this and I crumpall inside a moment.

Come on, says Devlin pattin me on the back. Keep movin.

I am alive, I thinks to myself. Gainst all the odds. I am alive.

We pulls and pushs ourselves throo so many cayves and tunnels that I do fayre lose count.

Cayves wi tiny spiders all legs and white lyke threads from a sheet.

Cayves wi a bad feel to them lyke somethin bad happend when you wunt lookin.

One wi dryde up bones o some big animal in a corner and a curvd bone lyke a sword. Bones so big I ent ever seen the lyke.

I dunt rytely kno how long we goes on for but we reetches the end o one cayve and all there is is water. Tis a dead end.

HOW DEEP IS IT? I SAYS LOOKIN INTO MY REFLEKSHUN FLICK FLICKRIN IN THE CANDUL LYTE.

I see me lookin back. Thin. Tired. A dark lyne down one cheek. The water black as a mirror.

I look at Devlin.

Rest or go on? I says. We been movin for an ayge.

We ent got no food, he says.

But a body can replenish wi sleep carnt it? I says. Cos if this is too deep, if tis truly a dead end an we got to go back, we needs all the energy we can get.

Fyve more matchiss, he says. Tis all.

I kno, I says.

He looks at me and thinks.

Alrtye, he says. We rest.

I find a smooth bit on the floor to curl up on and he dos the sayme. His back to my back, keepin in the warmth.

He blows out the lyte.

We lies there in the darkness, silence wrappd round us.

Devlin, I whispers and I feels him shift behind me. What happens when we get out o here? Where will we go?

You can come live wi me if you lyke Newt, he says. Tis only fayre I help you lyke you helpd me.

I think about this, about how all things seem both possible and impossible, and I smyles to myself.

I thawt you was the Devil when you turnd up, I says. Lyke your nayme was a warnin.

He grunts.

I dunt rytely kno how Ill be topside, I says. I dunt barely remember things fore Bearmouth.

Youre strong Newt, he says. Strongest person I ever did kno. Yule be ryte as rain back up there.

We lies there in silence for a bit.

I am a murderer, I says.

Devlin snorts. No you ent. Twas self defence, Walsh wuld o killd you and we both knos it. Besides, he says, we did free all o Bearmouth.

We did, I says. Sayve those men that got crushd in the crowd.

Twas not our fawlt Newt, he says. You must remember that. A mob o men will act diffrent to single folk. Twas not our fawlt. How many more wuld o died down the mine if we hadunt dun what we did?

That much tis true, I says.

Alryte, he says.

I thinks about it a moment. Alryte, I says.

I lay there thinkin. And I want to say it. So I do. I must. If I say it out loud then it is real.

I ent who you think I am, I says.

How dyou meen? he says.

I ent a lad arfter all, I says.

A man you meen? he says.

No, I says. I thinks to myself for a moment. Twill be the first time I have sed it out loud.

I ent a lad at all, I says. Thomas, he did hide the truth for many years. I ent a lad at all see, I am a gel.

But there ent no wimmin down the mines, he says.

I kno, I says. Tis why Thomas lied, keep me sayfe see.

Youre a gel? he says. Puzzld.

I am a gel, I says. And it feels funny lyke sayin it out

240

loud. So I larfs. I am a gel, I says. I am a gel, I says again louder.

And he starts larfin too. Youre a gel, he says and I shouts it.

I am Newt, I shouts, hearin it echo. I am Newt and I am a gel.

I larf and he larfs. I larf til I am helpless, til I feel tears o murth down my cheeks.

I am a gel, I say. Whisperin. I am a gel.

Devlin sniffs. Back still to myne.

Well you myte be a gel but youre still the brayvest person I ever did meet. And you will always be my best frend.

Tis a long time arfter that when sleep finally comes.

I am Newt. And I am a gel.

And it dunt sound so bad arfter all.

WHEN I WAYKES, DEVLIN IS GONE FROM BEHIND ME. I hears a tricklin in the corner and I kno that he dos answer a call o nayture.

Newt, he says. You awayke?

I am, I says. I been thinkin too. I need to see Ma when I get out. See her and see shes alryte and stuff. But . . .

But what? he says.

Well I ent too shore where she is see. Where the farm is. The nayme o the villidge and all. And Newt Coombes, well it ent my nayme really is it?

What you sayin Newt?

Well, can I really come and live wi you? Cos wi Ma, there ent much room see and if you had spayce . . . I kno Im anuvver mouth to feed and—

Corse, he says. I sed it and I ment it too. We will manidge. Weve manidged this far eh?

He opens his tin, strykes a match and lytes a stump o candul.

Fore more matchiss left, I say.

He nods.

I feels hungree and my belly dos rumble.

Ill go first, I says. Im a better swimmer.

Shore? he says and I nod.

I taykes off my hevvy boots, still wet. Peels off my socks. He looks away as I taykes off my shirt and trowsers leevin just my unders.

Im reddy, I says.

He holds the lyte up, still lookin away and I walks into the water. Slowly slowly feelin the chill o it on my skin.

It gets deep fast and I gasp as I near go under.

Reddy, I says.

Good luck, he says.

And I taykes a deep breath and then I dives.

I KEEPS MY EYES OPEN MAYKIN THE MOST O THE LYTE FROM THE CANDUL WAY ABOVE ME. Tis deep water but cleer.

I sees a dark patch low down and I dives towards it. Tis a tunnel. I come back up and tells Devlin but I dunt wayte for his answer fore I taykes one big deep breath and am down again and swimmin towards it.

Tis wyde enuff to swim throo comftablee and I go harf along it fore my lungs are fayre to burstin. As I go to turn I sees a flicker o lyte and I swims towards it even tho I ent shore whevver I am dreamin or seein somethin real.

My lungs go flat and I can feel my eyes goin as the air is pushd out o me but then Im out.

I heeve the air in deeply and it dos tayste so sweete.

Lyke flowers and shuggar and bein spinky clene arfter a barth.

I looks around. I am in a cayve but it ent a full cayve. There is a tree growin all green and leeves ryte throo a hole in the roof and up up.

I looks up at the sky behind the tree and it must needs be nyte as there ent no sun and tis dark still but there is a silver cloud ryte there as I looks up and tis so bryte tis lyke my eyes are fayre sore. And I kno a moon is behind it and I looks away for fear o bein blinded by it.

Tis lyke I am new born. And I carnt help myself. I cryes wi the sheer joy o it as the white bryteness dos wash over me.

Tis only when I get my breath back and dryes my eyes

that I realize I must go back. Devlin is not such a strong swimmer as me and twill be harder for him.

It dos tayke three goes fore he manidges to mayke it out. I has to harf pull him throo. I heeves him out onto the rocks as the moonlyte shines into the cayve. He lies on his back as we gets our breath back.

Tis lyke lectrick, I says blink blinkin at it.

Devlin coffs and coffs and then I realize he is larfin.

We mayde it, he says larfin. We mayde it.

We gathers our breath back for who knos how long.

I got to go back, I says. I kno my boots ent the best but theyre all I got.

Devlin goes to get up but I stops him.

Ill get yours and all, I says.

Dunt be long, he says and I grins at him.

You dunt even kno a faster swimmer than me eh, I says and he larfs.

I have to do it in two goes, the boots are hevvy and drag me down, tis hard work but I dos it. I rests a while at the base o the tree whilst Devlin wrings out the sodden wet clothes, empteein the boots o water and busyin himself tyin the clothes into two bundles wi the boot layces as I catches my breath. It feels lyke but a moment and he is dun.

Alryte? he says and I nod. Come on then, says Devlin and he gives me my clothes and boots all tied up wi a neat loop to carry em by.

I throw em over my sholder and we starts lookin for footholds in the tree.

We climbs up, our unders still wet from the swim, branches in my hand ruff and scratchee. Leeves brushin gainst my skin lyke ticklin me. The taste o fresh air in my lungs as we climbs up up the tree out o the cayve and towards the lyte. We are tired and hungree, still wet and harf nayked and our boots and clothes feel hevvy as we drags them up behind us, harf cawt on branches.

As we nears the surfiss, I reetches up and grasps the edge o the openin. Grass. Beneath my fingers for the first time in an ayge. Tis wet wi nyte dew. I grab the ground and heeves myself out onto it, diggin my fingers into the soil and tastin the air as I do so.

I crawls forwud a little way from the cayve openin, nees on grass and Devlin crawls out next to me, harf sobbin.

I sees trees in the distance gainst the lyte o the moon.

I sees hills and outside and I cryes wi joy and puzzlement and relief.

I am fayre worn out and I collapses onto my back, feelin the damp grass pricklin ruff underneeth my skin. Theres a spyders web jewlld lyke the most preshus thing by my hand. I reetches out and touches it.

I breethes it all in. The dampness o the grass, so fresh and clene. Tis sweete and bryte and new, lyke happyness. A bird hoots in the distance and the wind brushes the trees. A breeze runs along my skin lyke kindness.

We lays there, next to each uvver soakin it all in. My eyes slowly gettin used to the bryteness o the moon even tho tis not a full one yet.

You sed once to me that it taykes one person to start a revolushun, I says. But that ent all is it?

Tis, he says. It took you.

No, I says. Taykes more than one. One to start it but uvvers to make it happen.

He smyles and taykes my hand in his.

We lies there for a moment underneeth the stars twink

twinklin in the sky. And it dos remind me o all the canduls o Bearmouth just lyke Thomas sed.

Come on, I says as I gets to my feet and pulls him up.

Where to? he says.

Freedom, I says. Remember. And one day, tis sed, the Mayker will give us a sine, I says.

> We will all be foregivven
> And we will rise up to the land
> And the lyte that the Mayker holds there in his parm
> Will be givern to all of us
> And all shall prosper in this life and the next.

Amen, I says.

Amen, says Devlin.

And we walk hand in hand in the pale white moonlyte to the beginnins of a new world.

ACKNOWLEDGMENTS

All writers will tell you that they've been writing for years, which, certainly in my case, is true enough. I've been lucky enough to have a small and invaluable support network that has encouraged me over the years and without which *Bearmouth* would probably not exist.

The team at Writing West Midlands has been incredible—I have no idea if the equivalent exists in the US but if it does and you're an aspiring writer, find your local group, treasure the people in it and give them cake. Thanks to Jonathan, Emma, Heddwen and Lovely Liv for hot beverages and invaluable support.

In spring 2018, I was lucky enough to win the Bridge Awards/Moniack Mhor Emerging Writer award and am indebted to the team behind it. A confidence boost at a time when I needed it most, it's meant that I've been able to have priceless writing time on retreats. Thank you, you glorious bunch!

Thank you to my parents who have encouraged my creativity at every turn and to my "twin," Hannah Khalil, for being amazing over so many years, I would never have made it here without you. Thank you, too, to the marvelous Katy Moran for invaluable advice and editing tips early on and to Rachel Buchanan for feedback, philosophical rants and long walks. Thanks to Simon Bolton for geeky giggles, to Sara-Jane Arbury for creative inspiration, to Caitlin for the MTE (Most Traveled Envelope), to the creative whirlwind that is Sandra Salter and to the ever awesome Jules and Mart for laughter, parties and support.

Thank you to the Ludville Massive—Sian, Iran, Imogen, Tom and Miche, Jean the Poet, Ashleigh, Dulcie and Aidann, Paul S., the Gin Pigs, Lyn, Shaun, Bruford, you are all marvelous. Thanks to Tobe for letting me borrow your name—and to Saffron, else she'll get furious she's not included. Thanks also to the E17 Official Support Network, particularly Lucy Franklin, Imogen Carter and Ali G. Thanks also to all the lovely folks who've championed this book far and wide, particularly Emma Finnigan, Maura, Thi, Ruth, Nick Pegg, Kiran, Maya, Brian, Gill, Lauren, and the Riot ladies.

I owe a particular debt of gratitude to Naomi Luland for being one of the earliest readers of *Bearmouth* and for having faith in me for more years than I can remember. Mate, I owe you one.

Although *Bearmouth* is a work of fiction, it is inspired by the real-life experiences of miners in Victorian times. Two books in particular had a significant influence, so much so that I named key characters in memory of them—B. L. Coombes's *These Poor Hands* and Ray Devlin's *Children of the Pits*.

Huge thanks to my dear friend and wonderful agent Anwen Hooson for always believing in me.

Massive thanks to the glorious story wizard Sarah Odedina, the best editor anyone could possibly wish for. I am indebted to the Amazing Adam Freudenheim at Pushkin Press for his faith in both me and in Newt's story. Big thanks also to the wider and super-supportive Pushkin family, particularly Elise, Poppy, India and the eagle-eyed Rory.

Thanks too to Yeti Lambregts and Allison Hellegers for being total stars.

Thank you to my amazing US team—I am so glad *Bearmouth* found the perfect home stateside! Thanks to Simon Boughton for being so welcoming, to Kristin Allard for unremitting cheerfulness and patience, to Beth Steidle for her sterling work and to the incredible Jon Gray for his stunning cover artwork.

And last but very much not least, thank you to my awesome other half, Rob, who makes it all worthwhile.